8.95

N

A

Embers
STORIES FOR A CHANGING WORLD

Edited by Ruth S. Meyers, Ph.D.; Beryle Banfield, Ed.D.; and
Jamila Gastón Colón

Lenore Ringler, Ph.D., Consultant

Developed by the Council on Interracial Books for Children
Supplementary Reading Comprehension Program, Grades 4-6

The Feminist Press
Old Westbury, New York

Council on Interracial Books for Children
New York, New York

A Project of the Women's Educational
Equity Act Program, United States
Department of Education

Developed by the Council on Interracial
Books for Children

These materials were developed under a grant to the Council on Interracial Books for Children from the U.S. Department of Health, Education and Welfare, Office of Education, under the auspices of the Women's Educational Equity Act. However, the opinions expressed herein do not necessarily reflect the position or policy of the Office of Education, and no official endorsement by the Office of Education should be inferred.

ACKNOWLEDGMENTS

Grateful acknowledgment is made of the following authors and publishers for permission to use and adapt copyrighted materials.

- Pantheon Books, a Division of Random House, Inc. for "Gloria Who Might Be My Best Friend," reprinted from **The Stories Julian Tells** by Ann Cameron, © 1981 by Ann Cameron.

- Eve Merriam for "Millie and Willie" from **There is No Rhyme for Silver** by Eve Merriam, copyright 1962 by Eve Merriam. Reprinted by permission of the author.

- Gay Bell for permission to print "Lawnmowers, Inc." by Gay Bell © 1981.

- The Dial Press for the text excerpt "Growin'" adapted from the book **Growin'** by Nikki Grimes. Copyright © 1977 by Nikki Grimes.

- Albert Whitman and Company for permission to adapt material from **All Kinds of Families** © 1976 by Norma Simon, illustrations © 1976 by Joe Lasker. Used with the permission of Albert Whitman and Company.

- The Asian American Bilingual Center for permission to reprint "Common Bond" by Kimi Narimatsu from **Sojourner IV**. Reprinted courtesy of Linda Wing and the Asian Writers Project, Berkeley High School, Berkeley, California.

- Scholastic, Inc., for "Sound of Sunshine, Sound of Rain," excerpt adapted from **Sound of Sunshine, Sound of Rain** by Florence Parry Heide. Copyright © 1979 by Florence Parry Heide. Reprinted by permission of Four Winds Press, a division of Scholastic, Inc. Originally published by Parents Magazine Press.

- New Seed Press and Inez Maury for **My Mother and I Are Growing Strong** by Inez Maury, copyright by New Seed Press, 1978. Used with permission of New Seed Press and Inez Maury © 1978. The story is available in a bilingual edition from New Seed Press, 1665 Euclid Avenue, Berkeley, CA 94709. Catalog available on request.

- Eve Merriam for "Color" from **It Doesn't Always Have to Rhyme** by Eve Merriam. Copyright © 1964 by Eve Merriam. Reprinted by permission of the author.

Continued on p. 172

Table of Contents

UNIT 1

FRIENDSHIP

Gloria Who Might Be My Best Friend

by Ann Cameron

If you have a girl for a friend, people find out and tease you. That's why I didn't want a girl for a friend — not until this summer, when I met Gloria.

It happened one afternoon when I was walking down the street by myself. My mother was visiting a friend of hers, and my brother Huey was visiting a friend of his. Huey's friend is five and so I think he is too young to play with. And there aren't any kids just my age. I was walking down the street feeling lonely.

A block from our house I saw a moving van in front of a brown house, and men were carrying in chairs and tables and bookcases and boxes full of I don't know what. I watched for a while, and suddenly I heard a voice right behind me.

"Who are you?"

I turned around and there was a girl in a yellow dress. She looked the same age as me. She had curly hair that was braided into two pigtails with red ribbons at the ends.

"I'm Julian," I said. "Who are you?"

"I'm Gloria," she said. "I come from Newport. Do you know where Newport is?"

I wasn't sure, but I didn't tell Gloria. "It's a town on the ocean," I said.

"Right," Gloria said. "Can you turn a cartwheel?"

She turned sideways herself and did two cartwheels on the grass.

I had never tried a cartwheel before, but I tried to copy Gloria. My hands went down in the grass, my feet went up in the air, and — I fell over.

I look at Gloria to see if she was laughing at me. If

she was laughing at me, I was going to go home and forget about her.

But she just looked at me very seriously and said, "It takes practice," and then I liked her.

"I know where there's a bird's nest in your yard," I said.

"Really?" Gloria said. "There weren't any trees in the yard, or any birds, where I lived before."

I showed her where a robin lives and has eggs. Gloria stood up on a branch and looked in. The eggs were small and pale blue. The mother robin squawked at us, and she and the father robin flew around our heads.

"They want us to go away," Gloria said. She got down from the branch, and went around to the front of the house and watched the moving men carry two rugs and a mirror inside. "Would you like to come over to my house?" I said.

"All right," Gloria said, "if it is all right with my mother." She ran in the house and asked.

It was all right, so Gloria and I went to my house, and I showed her my room and my games and my rock collection, and then I made strawberry Kool-Aid and we sat at the kitchen table and drank it.

"You have a red moustache on your mouth," Gloria said.

"You have a red moustache on your mouth, too," I said.

Gloria giggled, and we licked off the moustaches with our tongues.

"I wish you'd live here a long time," I told Gloria.

Gloria said, "I wish I would too."

"I know the best way to make wishes," Gloria said.

"What's that?" I asked.

"First you make a kite. Do you know how to make one?"

"Yes," I said, "I know how." I know how to make good kites, because my father taught me. We make them out of two crossed sticks and folded newspaper.

"All right," Gloria said, "that's the first part of making wishes that come true. So let's make a kite."

We went out into the garage, and spread out sticks and newspaper, and made a kite. I fastened on the kite string, and went to the closet and got rags for the tail.

"Do you have some paper and two pencils?" Gloria asked. "Because now we make the wishes."

I didn't know what she was planning, but I went in the house and got pencils and paper.

"All right," Gloria said. "Every wish you want to have come true you write on a long thin piece of paper. You don't tell me your wishes, and I don't tell you mine. If you tell, your wishes don't come true. Also, if you look at the other person's wishes, your wishes don't come true."

Gloria sat down on the garage floor again and started writing her wishes. I wanted to see what they were — but I went to the other side of the garage and wrote my own wishes instead. I wrote:

1. I wish I could have a cat.
2. I wish our fig tree would be the tallest in town.
3. I wish I'd be a great soccer player.
4. I wish I could ride in an airplane.
5. I wish Gloria would stay here and be my best friend.

I folded my five wishes in my fist and went over to Gloria. "How many wishes did you make?" Gloria asked.

"Five," I said. "How many did you make?"

"Two," Gloria said.

I wondered what they were.

"Now we put the wishes on the tail of the kite," Gloria said. "Every time we tie one piece of rag on the tail, we fasten a wish in the knot. You can put yours in first."

I fastened mine in, and then Gloria fastened in hers, and we carried the kite into the yard.

"You hold the tail," I told Gloria, "and I'll pull."

We ran through the back yard with the kite, passed the garden and the fig tree, and went into the open field beyond our yard.

The kite started to rise. The tail jerked heavily like a long white snake. In a minute the kite passed the roof of my house and was climbing toward the sun.

We stood in the open field, looking up at it. I was wishing I would get my wishes.

"I know it's going to work!" Gloria said.

"How do you know?"

"When we take the kite down," Gloria told me, "there shouldn't be one wish in the tail. When the wind takes all your wishes, that's when you know it's going to work."

The kite stayed up for a long time. We both held the string. The kite looked like a tiny black spot in the sun, and my neck got stiff from looking at it.

"Shall we pull it in?" I asked.

"All right," Gloria said.

We drew the string in more and more until, like a tired bird, the kite fell at our feet.

We looked at the tail. All our wishes were gone. Probably they were still flying higher and higher in the wind.

Maybe I would get a cat and get to be a good soccer player and have a ride in an airplane and own the tallest fig tree in town. And Gloria would be my best friend.

"Gloria," I said, "did you wish we would be friends?"

"You're not supposed to ask me that!" Gloria said.

"I'm sorry," I answered. But inside I was smiling. I guessed one thing Gloria wished for. I was pretty sure we would be friends.

MILLIE and WILLIE

by Eve Merriam

When
Millie and Dottie and Lottie
And Rita and Carmencita
All play ball
And Willie wants to play, too,
And they say
"Go away, you're a boy,
Go jump in the lake, bellyache!"
Then
Don't you agree with Willie
That girls are stupidly silly?

But
When Willie and Freddy and Teddy
and Juan and Don
Play ball
And Millie wants to play, too,
And they say
"Go away, you're a girl,
Go tell your mother she wants you,
You big fat skinny dunce you!"
Then
Don't you agree with Millie
That boys are stupidly silly?

Lawnmowers, Inc.

by Gay Bell

"What's the idea, stealing our lawn business?" Andy scowled at Jill.

"Sarah and I didn't steal your business," said Jill. "We didn't ask *all* the neighbors if we could mow their lawns this summer — just the Johnsons and the Hays and the Baldwins."

"Joe and I've mowed their lawns the last two summers," said Andy. "We just hadn't gotten around to asking if we could cut their yards this year. We need the money to buy new T-shirts for our baseball team!"

"Wear your old shirts," said Jill.

"They're full of holes!" Andy protested. "Would you want to play baseball with holes in your uniform?"

"I wouldn't know," said Jill. "You won't let Sarah and me play."

"You're mad about baseball!" said Andy. "So you took our lawns!"

"The truth is," said Jill, "Sarah and I need the money."

"What do you girls need money for?" Andy asked scornfully.

"That's for *us* to know." Jill started to walk away.

"Wait a minute!" Andy called. "I've got an idea! Tomorrow, you and Sarah cut Mrs. Baldwin's yard. Joe and I'll cut Mr. Hedrick's. Each team will start mowing at the same time. Whichever team finishes first, wins. The prize will be — !" Andy chuckled. "The winning team takes over the lawn business for the whole neighborhood."

"The Baldwins' and the Hays' and the Johnsons' yard too?"

"Right!" said Andy. "But — " He raised his eyebrows. "If you think you'd lose, you won't want to try it."

Jill stamped her foot. "We'll win! We'll have *all* the lawn mowing business!"

"Fat chance!" said Andy. "Be ready at ten o'clock tomorrow. Bring one lawnmower and one set of clippers. One person mows. One person trims. Same lawnmower, same clippers used for the whole job. Shake on it?"

"Shake!" said Jill.

By noon the next day sweat dripped down the girls' faces. Jill hollered to Sarah over the roar of the lawnmower. "Andy and Joe got drinks from the hose three times!"

"Don't count," yelled Sarah. "Trim!"

Jill finished the side yard. She heard Sarah's lawnmower stop. "Don't stop mowing!" she hollered.

"They'll beat us."

"It's out of gas! I've got to fill it."

"Hurry!" said Jill.

"I'm hurrying," said Sarah.

Jill rubbed her back. Trimming was hard work. She hollered across the street. "O.K. if Sarah and I switch jobs?"

Andy hollered back. "As long as you use the same lawnmower and clippers!"

"How about lunch?" yelled Joe.

"You can go," yelled Jill. "We'll keep working."

"Naw!" Joe scowled. "We're not hungry."

Carefully, Sarah poured gasoline into the tank. She pulled the starter cord again and again.

"Let me try," said Jill.

The lawnmower would not start.

"What'll we do?" wailed Jill. "We have to win! We've got to earn that money."

"Get *your* lawnmower," suggested Sarah.

"I can't," said Jill. "We have to use the same lawnmower, same pair of clippers."

"A silly rule!" said Sarah.

"I know," said Jill. "But I agreed to it."

"Maybe they'll let us change the rules," said Sarah. "We can't help it if this lawnmower won't start."

They hollered across the street and asked if they could switch lawnmowers.

"No!" the boys called. They came across the street. "You'll have to fix it."

"We don't know how!" said Jill. Quickly, she wiped away a tear.

"You'll have to learn," said Andy. "We'd give you some advice if we weren't leaving for lunch."

"I can't wait to get that hamburger!" Joe rubbed his stomach. "See you later!"

"We've got plenty of time," Andy said loudly. "They'll *never* fix that lawnmower. We've won for sure!"

Joe and Andy got on their bicycles. They rode away.

"They're right," said Jill. "I can't fix a lawnmower."

"My mom could fix it," said Sarah. "But she gets home from work too late." She pulled her ear. "While the boys are gone, we could use your lawnmower."

Jill thought for a minute. She shook her head. "That wouldn't be honest. We have to fix this one."

"We could read the instruction book," said Sarah. "I know where it is."

The girls pushed the lawnmower as fast as they could to Sarah's garage. Sarah got the instruction book. The girls bent over the lawnmower. They took out the air filter. It was clean.

"What can we try now?" asked Jill. She looked at her watch. "We've got to hurry! The boys may be back any minute. They'll start mowing!"

Sarah turned to page five of the instructions. "I'll check the spark plug."

Carefully, Sarah pulled off the spark plug wire. She found a wrench and started trying to loosen the spark plug. "It's stuck!" she said. "There! Got it! Now, what?"

She turned to page six. "Hand me that rag." Sarah cleaned a gob of black goop off the plug. "That's better! Now, if I can get it back!" She bent over the lawnmower. She pulled on the starter.

Nothing happened.

"It's not going to start!" Jill moaned. "We'll lose for sure!"

"We can't!" Sarah said stubbornly. "We've got to keep our lawn business. We've got to earn that money." She pulled on the cord. The motor was as silent as an unplugged TV.

"Try again," Jill said. She crossed her fingers. If they lost their lawn mowing business, it would be *her* fault. *Why* had she made such a stupid bargain?

Sarah yanked on the cord. The motor coughed. She pulled again. The mower started! The girls hugged each other. They rushed out of the garage with the lawnmower. Quickly, they looked across the street.

"Where could the boys be?" asked Jill.

"Don't know," said Sarah. "Let's hurry!"

They started on the Baldwins' back yard. Jill

mowed. Sarah trimmed. At last they finished. They were so tired they could hardly push the lawnmower to the front. Anxiously, Jill looked for the boys. For the last hour she'd expected to hear them yell, "We beat you!"

"Maybe they finished mowing and went home," said Sarah.

"Not a chance!" said Jill. "They wouldn't leave without bragging they'd won."

Just then the girls saw Andy and Joe on their bicycles. Andy was sucking on a straw. Joe was eating a pickle.

"Sorry, we don't have anything left," said Joe.

"And we're sorry you didn't get your lawnmower fixed," said Andy. "You ready to give up?"

For a minute Jill didn't say anything. Laughter rose inside her like a volcano.

"We didn't mean to stay so long," said Joe, "but we were hungry!"

Andy snickered. "And we *knew* you girls would be busy trying to fix your lawnmower!"

"It's fixed!" said Sarah.

"We won!" Jill hollered. "We beat you fair and square!"

Andy looked shocked. "You girls fixed the lawnmower? You finished mowing the Baldwins' yard?"

"Right!" said Sarah. "Now, you keep *your* part of the bargain."

Andy looked so sad Jill almost felt sorry for him. He cleared his throat. "All right. You and Sarah get to mow all the lawns this summer." He turned to Joe. "Now, we can't buy T-shirts for our baseball team."

Joe sighed. "Do us one favor. Tell us what's so important you and Sarah need the lawn money for."

The girls whispered. At first Jill shook her head. Then she nodded.

"We have a deal to offer," she said. "We'll tell you why we need the money if you'll agree to our plan. Sarah and I'll keep the Hays', the Johnsons', and the Baldwins' yard. You and Joe can mow the other lawns."

"We don't want to mow them *all*," said Sarah. "We wouldn't have time to play."

Big smiles spread across the boys' faces.

"You bet!" said Andy. "It's a deal!"

"We're going to buy a shade tree for the park," Jill said. "For our Scout project."

"A *big* shade tree!" said Sarah. "We'll plant it next to the picnic bench so people can have shade for their picnics."

"I have another idea!" said Jill.

The boys groaned.

"Let's do our lawns together this summer! We'll call ourselves 'Lawnmowers, Inc.' After Sarah and I buy our shade tree, we'll buy T-shirts for *all* the team."

"I'll pitch. Sarah can catch," said Jill.

Andy started to shake his head.

"Lawnmowers, Inc." Jill said firmly.

Andy nodded. They shook hands.

GROWIN'
by Nikki Grimes

"You're new, aren't you. Yo-lan-da?" He stretched my name out so that I could tell he was making fun of me.

"Don't call me Yolanda," I said boldly. "My name is Pump. And don't you forget it." I was trying real hard to sound tough so that he would leave me alone. But he didn't believe me.

"I'll call you Yolanda as much as I feel like it. What are you goin' to do about it?" he said, and he was looking mean. Well, I knew I wasn't going to get out of a fight, so I put my books down on the ground and tried not to shake so much from being scared.

Then I made myself look him in the eye.

"If you call me Yo-lan-da again, I'll push you, that's what." He still didn't believe me.

"I dare you," he said. Everybody knew you were scared if you backed down from a dare, and they would pick on you for the rest of your life. So I pushed him as hard as I could. I waited for him to push back, but he didn't.

"I dare you to do it again," he said. My knees weren't knocking exactly, they just rattled a little. But I pushed him again.

"I dare you to do it again," he said. So I pushed him a third time and waited for him to kill me. Instead he bent down and picked up my books from the ground. Then he broke out in a big sunshine smile.

"My name is Jim Jim," he said. "Welcome to the block, Pump."

One day I'd been wanting to go for a swim all day, but Jim Jim was afraid of the water so I hadn't said anything about it. But my clothes were sticking all to me, so I changed my mind. I took off my shoes and stuck my toes in first to see if it was good and cold. It was.

"What you doin?" asked Jim Jim, plopping down on a rock.

"What's it look like?" I said.

Jim Jim picked up a piece of stick and started drawing something in the dirt. He looked up serious.

"You know you ain't supposed to swim here."

"Who said?"

"Your mama."

"Mama ain't here," I said.

"The sign then." He pointed to a green-and-white painted wood sign sticking out of the dirt.

"Last week you said I couldn't read."

Jim Jim rolled his eyes and went back to his drawing.

"Anyway," I teased, "you just said that cause you're

scared to get in yourself."

Jim Jim's face puffed up red, but he just kept on drawing. I jumped in.

"Wheeeee!" I screamed. I stuck my head under the water and stayed there till I couldn't hold my breath any longer. I came up splashing and slapping the water with the stiff palm of my hand. Jim Jim wasn't in the water, but he sure was good and wet by the time I finished.

"Come on in." I laughed. "The water's fine." Jim Jim just shook his head no. He was busy digging up worms to throw at me cause he knew how icky I thought they were. That's when the idea hit me.

The water was only up to my waist. I walked out a little farther and started splashing and coughing at the same time.

"Help! Help!" I screamed. Jim Jim looked up.

"Help! Help!" I screamed again.

Jim Jim shot up and took two steps to the edge of the river and stopped. He looked down at the water and I could see the fear in his eyes. Then he looked at me as if he was discovering me for the first time. I coughed and spluttered and went under. When I came up the next time, Jim Jim was waistdeep in the river coming to me fast. I was still flapping around, but I had stopped coughing. Jim Jim was up to his shoulders. I stood up straight in the water and smiled. Jim Jim stopped dead. The water was up to his neck. He looked down at the river that had swallowed up more than half his body. He opened his mouth, but nothing came out. I couldn't hold it back. I laughed for all the world to hear.

"Cat got your tongue, Jim Jim?" I said.

"You ain't drownin'," he said. "You ain't drownin', Pump." Jim Jim said it over and over again to make himself believe it, and there I was laughing till the fear came back to his eyes.

"Aw, Jim Jim," I said. "Don't be afraid. It's only water. Come on." I took a step forward toward him. He took a step back.

"Don't be like that, Jim Jim," I called. "I bet you're a real good swimmer, too," I said. He took another step back and went under. I saw him waving and kicking and thought he was playing for a minute. Then I walked to the spot where he was standing and got pulled under too. There's a point in the river where the current switches. Jim Jim had walked right into it and I had followed. Now the river was pulling every which way and filling our lungs to bursting and taking us deeper. Jim Jim was flapping and kicking and spitting out water. He wasn't swimming. Jim Jim really couldn't swim. He was going to save me from drowning and he couldn't even swim. And neither could I.

I felt around in the water for Jim Jim's hand. I found it and held on to it like life. It was life, Jim Jim's hand.

"Stand up! Stand up!" I yelled. "Pull, Jim Jim!" Jim Jim pulled. He stood up and was pulled back down. He got on his feet once more and dug his toes into the sandy earth and fought the current. He held my hand and he pulled. Again he was dragged down. His head bobbed up, his eyes shooting from left to right along the riverbank. He turned to look at me. The fear had gone from his eyes.

"It's O.K., Pump," he said. "It's O.K." Then he disappeared underneath the water. He'd felt something. I didn't know what, but I kept holding on. Jim Jim had been under the river for a long time. I started worrying. Was he all right? Nobody could hold his breath that long.

I felt a tug on my hand. Jim Jim was moving and he

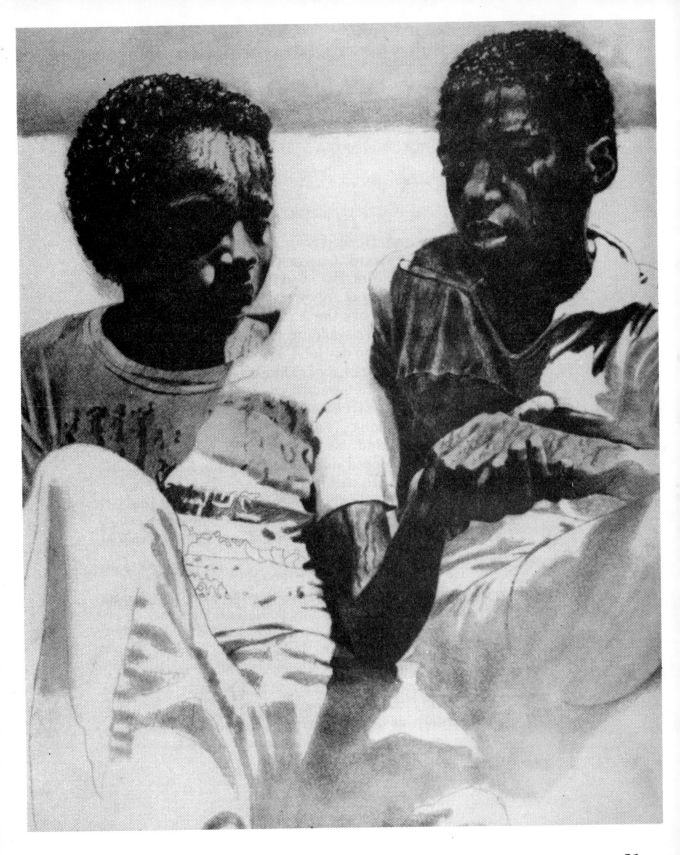

was pulling me. He still hadn't come up for air, but he was moving forward. One step at a time. And he was pulling me with him. His head finally came up out of the water. The water was only waist deep now, but only Jim Jim's head was above the water. He was leaning to one side and seemed to be holding on to something. When we were almost back on dry land, I could see what he'd been holding on to. A tree root. Thank God for tree roots, I thought. My eyes followed the root from where we stood in the water to the tree itself. The tree was just near the edge of the riverbank. That's what Jim Jim had felt when he turned to me and said, "It's O.K., Pump. It's O.K."

Jim Jim plopped down on the ground, pulling me down with him. He still held my hand. I stared down at it. Warm, brown, strong. Jim Jim's hand. It was life.

We sat quiet, catching our breath, easing out the fear and the shock in long deep sighs. Jim Jim broke the silence.

"Hey, Pump," he said. "I thought you could swim."

I laughed inside, and the deep-down laugh pushed its way to my mouth and out and spilled all over that riverbank.

That's when Jim Jim and I became friends. That's when I told him that I wrote poetry and he told me that he liked to draw. And that's when I finally told Jim Jim about Daddy and about how it was with Mama and me. The testing was over. The trust was true and setting in, and we settled down to being as close as two sides of one coin. Yeah.

UNIT 2
FAMILIES ARE IMPORTANT

ALL KINDS *of* FAMILIES

by Norma Simon

A family is YOU. And the people who live with you,
and love you, and take care of you.
  There are all kinds of families,
  but your own is the one you know best.

Families come in all sizes,
BIG FAMILIES, MIDDLE SIZED FAMILIES, LITTLE
FAMILIES.

Families come in all ages, too.
  Young families with young children.
  Middle-aged families with teen-aged children.
  Old families with grownup children
  and grandchildren.

Families come with all kinds of people, different sizes,
  different ages. They make all kinds of families.

A family is people who belong together.
    Like husbands and wives and their children.
    Like mothers and children . . .
    Like fathers and children.
    Like grandparents and grandchildren.

People who live together, love
together,
    fight together and make up, work
    and play with each other, laugh
    and cry and live under one roof
    together . . . They are a family.

What's *special* about a family? It's
    the feeling you have about each
    other from living in the same
    place, sharing good times and
    bad times . . . growing together.

A family can be a mother, a father,
    and children who are growing up.
A family can be a mother and her
    children, living, loving, working and sharing.
A family can be a father and his children,
    living, loving, working and sharing.
A big sister or a big brother
    taking care of other children . . . can be a family.
And a father and a mother together,
    their children grownup and away . . . can be a family.

Children who live far away send letters. They write,
    "I'll be home soon.
    Can hardly wait to see everybody."

They telephone, too.
    "Hi, Mom! Hi, Dad! How are you?
    I'll be home for the holidays."

Families like to come together, for holidays, birthdays, a
wedding, for sad times and for happy times.

When families get together, they talk a lot, they eat a lot,
they laugh a lot.

When everyone has said good-bye, the home feels empty.

Family people have family names.
Like mother, father, sister, brother, son and daughter.
Like cousin, aunt, uncle, niece, nephew,
    grandmother and grandfather.

All your relatives and relations have these family names.

When families go visiting, you hear many family names.
    Names like Aunt Susan and Uncle Ed.
    Names for different grandparents,
    like Grandma Hall and Granny Baker.

Some children have many relatives and relations.
    Almost too many to remember.
Some children have only a few, and it's easy
    to name every one.

Can you name your Aunts?
    Uncles? Grandparents?

Do you know their first names?
You are part of your family,
    of the caring . . .
    and the sharing
    and the loving.

From the time when you're a tiny baby,
    when you're growing up . . . . all grown up.
All your life, wherever you live,
    YOU are a part of a family.

A family is YOU and the people who live with you.
That's one part of your family.

Some people in your family may live in different
places. They are still your family.

Part of your family lives far away,
in another city . . . in another part of town,
or nearby . . . in a different house.

You visit them. They visit you.
And you know that they are family people:
aunts, uncles, cousins, grandparents.

A mother or a father may live in a different place,
   a place not with their children.
No matter how near or how far, you are still part
   of the same family.

Some families live in the same home for a long time.
Other families move from place to place.

But in a family home, there are things people like
   to keep around them: family pictures, a special chair,
      books . . . pets . . . toys.
They take these things from one home to another.

When you are grown up, you may begin your own family,
      a new family . . . a young family.
When a mother and a father have a child or adopt a child,
      a new family begins.

And the *new* family becomes a part of all the *old* ones:
      Part of the mother's family.
      Part of the father's family.

People in old and new families like to tell each other
      where they are, what they are doing.
They send letters, postcards, birthday cards.

Dear Amy,

   I wish we could get together
more often. It was wonderful
to see you at Thanksgiving.
   Thank you for a lovely day.
   All the best,
   Aunt Ruth

A letter for you has YOUR last name on it.
Lots of persons in a family share the same last name.
But, maybe, not all of them.

And some people who aren't even in the same family
    have the same last name. That happens!

Families last a long . . . long . . . time.
    New babies are born or are adopted.
    Some people die.
    There are new husbands, new wives,
    comings together, and goings apart.

There are changes, but families go on.
Families share special stories that family people
    like to hear.
The stories make everyone part of the big family.

Are there stories told in your family?
    Maybe there are stories about you, something you
    did.
    Maybe you hear the same stories over and over.
    Some day . . . you'll tell them, too.

Some uncles tell stories, funny stories, silly stories.
Stories about mischief they did.
Stories about adventures they had.
Stories all about people you know.
And aunts tell you more stories, ones they know.

Families like to tell stories many times.
    The old stories are new to the youngest children.
    They listen and want to hear them again.
Funny stories, sad stories, part of growing up in a family.

Sometimes members of a family
    don't see each other for a long time.
Maybe it's because they live too far away.
Or because families have fights and don't agree.
Maybe people are working,
    and there is no time to be together.

But when a family *does* come together
after a long time, they say things like:
    "Oh, how the children have grown!"
    "Your hair is still so curly . . ."
    "It's *good* to be together again."
    "I'd know your girl anywhere.
    I remember when you looked like that."
And the family feeling is all around them
    like a strong, invisible circle.

When *you* need help, your family helps you.
When your family needs help, *you* help them.
People in a family help each other
    and try to take care of each other.

Yes, families are for caring . . . loving . . . sharing . . .
    far or near, big or little . . . all kinds of families.

All kinds of families —
    and yours is one of them.

Your family is always part of you.
You are always part of it.

A family is a special part of your life.

COMMON BOND

My mother,
not so close are we,
yet we share a common bond,
    a goal,
    a unity.
Not because she is my mother,
and I her daughter
But because we are both Asian,
in a world of prejudices and hate.
We need to stay together as one,
    to survive,
    to love,
    to live.
We need to fight for our rights.
My mother,
she lives in a world as a person.
She fights for what she knows is right.
She works so hard to give me what I need.
    I give her in return what she needs,
       love,
       peace,
       understanding,
       and the will to live as an Asian
         and person.
Together, my mother and I are one.

by Kimi Narimatsu

My Mother and I Are Growing Strong

By Inez Maury

MY MOTHER GROWS FLOWERS

Here I am, Emilita, working with my mother, Lupe, in Ms. Stubblebine's flower garden. We've just finished trimming the roses, the flowers my mother loves the most, and now we're weeding the sunflowers, which are my favorites. Sunflowers are so happy, growing vast and strong by the high wall and turning their faces all day long to the sun. It's good we like flowers because we have to work hard these months while Daddy's in prison. Ms. Stubblebine says we make the garden as pretty as he did when he was her gardener. My mother shakes her head and says no, but she smiles just the same.

MY MOTHER KEEPS SECRETS

She never tells the special secrets her women friends tell her. That's good. But it's bad that the biggest secret of all she is keeping from Daddy. He doesn't know that she kept all his gardening jobs going when he left us this spring. He thinks his wife shouldn't work. He says he loves her and wants to be good to her, but he thinks she should stay home.

MY MOTHER KNOWS MACHINES

Our truck broke down as if it knew Daddy was gone. But a neighbor showed my mother how to fix it. She found that the insides of machines are really simple. She learned all about spark plugs and pistons, and yesterday she surprised another gardener by fixing his power mower. She tells me I don't need to lose my temper when my electric train won't go. She shows me how to get it racing around the tracks in a minute.

MY MOTHER SAYS BE FAIR

She says you have to be fair to people and you have to be fair to yourself, too. If some kid comes into the park and starts throwing sand or grabbing your swing, you fight back. Even Daddy fights if he has to. When he caught some men towing his truck away, he yelled at them to stop. They swore and said he hadn't paid on the truck and shoved a bill at him.

"Hey!" my daddy said, "this bill is for José Hernandez. My name is José GONZALES."

"Okay, okay," one man said, "Hernandez, Gonzales, you're all thieves, anyway."

Daddy gave that man such a punch that he fell down and his head hit the sidewalk. And the ambulance had to come. I thought Daddy was right to fight, but the judge didn't and put Daddy in prison for a year. He may get out sooner, maybe next month, if something called a parole board will let him. We hope so. All we can think of is getting him home. My mother may get good news when she visits him next week. I wish she would take me, but she says a prison is too sad for children. I say why is it worse for children than for grown-ups?

MY MOTHER USES WORMS

Yummy! Yesterday she came home with an ice-cream carton. But when I opened it, up popped hundreds of curly red earthworms. I almost dropped them. My mother laughed more than she has for a long time. One wiggled down and started to play with me, but I had to close it back tight in the box. I was happy and sad when we dumped them in Ms. Stubblebine's garden this morning — happy because the worms were free and could make the garden airy and rich, but sad to lose that one worm who was so friendly.

MY MOTHER CAN CHANGE HER MIND

She let me visit Daddy after all. A prison is terrible, all high walls and gates. We went through gates and gates and finally got into a big room filled with visitors. It smelled so scary. Then a guard called our name and put us in a smaller room with glass cages. Daddy was sitting inside one of them. He seemed so pale and strange I started to cry, but he frowned so I stopped. He reached through a little opening and squeezed my hand. We talked about things like the summer weather. I almost told him how high his sunflowers were climbing, but then I remembered the secret. Finally, he told us that the parole board said he couldn't go home yet. That's when my mother began to cry. I did, too, but Daddy didn't. I've always wondered why men don't cry. He just got paler. Then the guard made us go. I'll have to think of something funny to do for our next visit — that is, if my mother will let me go again.

MY MOTHER SAYS WE'RE HEALTH NUTS

"You're happy if you're healthy," she keeps saying, so we eat sunflower seeds and do push-ups and headstands together. Some people think we're crazy, but we don't care. You should taste our salads. We can't grow much in our apartment, but we have onions and radishes and cilantro in our window boxes and on the fire escape. My mother is getting so healthy she can shovel a ton of dirt and not puff. I'm one of the fastest runners in my class, even as fast as the Flynn twins.

MY MOTHER LIKES FUN

We have lots of best times, like when we have cousins to dinner or take the Flynn twins out in the truck to pick up wild berries. The very best times, though, are when she and I snuggle in Daddy's big chair and look at my storybooks or flower catalogs. Sometimes, even though it makes her sad, she looks at pictures of Daddy. If she cries, I stand on my head, and she has to laugh.

MY MOTHER IS GETTING BRAVE

One night after we went to bed, we heard a noise by the fire escape and saw a man trying to break into our apartment. I was scared, but my mother grabbed her garden hoe and went right to the window.

"Get out of here and don't come back!" she yelled.

The man disappeared. My mother surprised herself to be so brave.

MY MOTHER IS WISE

She said yes, I could visit the prison again. Ms. Stubblebine made a big bouquet of roses for me to take, but my mother said no, flowers weren't allowed. I wondered what I could do to make Daddy cheerful. Stand on my head? My mother said no again. Well, if he couldn't have flowers, maybe he could have vegetables. I made a pretty bouquet of our window box radishes. They looked so happy with their round faces looking up from the lacy collar of their leaves. My mother couldn't say no again. The guard let me through with them, but when Daddy saw them, instead of laughing, he began to cry. I guess men do cry. I thought I'd cry, too, but a smile came on him

and he said the parole board was going to free him next week. My mother screamed and threw her arms so fast that she cracked her fingers on the glass.

"Wonderful, Daddy," I said, jumping up and down. "We'll get you home and show you how tall we've made Ms. Stubblebine's sunflowers grow. They're almost to the sun!"

Daddy's eyebrows went up.

"Yes," said my mother, looking glad that I'd let her secret out, "we've worked hard in your gardens."

"What?" Daddy said. "Cousin Alfonso was supposed to take over my jobs."

"I didn't need him," said my mother, "I have the best gardener ever — Emilita."

"Well," said my father, "when I get home, you won't work any more."

"We'll see," my mother said very quietly. I held my breath. Then a funny thing happened. Daddy smiled at her. Then he looked at me and winked! Right through the bright glass of the cage, I could feel his love come out at us.

Sound of Sunshine, Sound of Rain

by Florence Parry Heide

Part I

IT MUST BE MORNING, for I hear the morning voices.

I have been dreaming of a sound that whispers, *Follow me. Follow me,* but not in words. I follow the sound up and up until I feel I am floating in the air.

Now I am awake, and I listen to the voices.

My mother's voice is warm and soft as a pillow.

My sister's voice is little and sharp and high, like needles flying in the air.

I do not listen to the words but to the sound. Low, high, low, high, soft, hard, soft, hard, and then the sounds coming together at the same time and making a new sound. And with it all, the sharp sounds of my sister's heels putting holes in what I hear.

Then I hear the slamming of kitchen drawers and the banging of pans and there is no more talking.

My bed is in the living room. I reach out to feel whether my mother has laid my clothes on the chair beside my bed. They are there, and I feel the smoothness and the roughness of them.

I reach under the chair to find which shoes my mother has put there. They are my outside shoes, not my slippers, so today must be a warm day. Maybe I can go to the park. I tap my good luck song on the wall beside my bed.

I put my feet on the floor and feel the cool wood and curl my toes against it.

Then it is four steps to the table, then around the table, touching the chairs, and then seven steps to the window. I put my cheek against the window, and I can feel the warm sun. Now I am sure I can go to the park if my sister has time to take me on her way to study.

I take my clothes into the bathroom, and I wash and dress there. Hot water, cold water, soapy water, plain water, loud water, still water. Then I make sure I have turned the faucets tight. I make sure I have buttoned all of my buttons the right way, or my sister will be cross, and maybe not have time to take me to the park.

I tap my good luck song against the door before I open it.

When I open the door, I hear the voices again. My sister's voice is like scissors cutting away at my mother's voice.

I sit at the table, and my mother gives me my breakfast. I breathe on the hot chocolate so I can feel it on my face coming back warm. I drink just a little at a time so I can keep holding the warm cup.

"Eat while it's hot," says my sister to me, loud.

"Does he have to be so slow?" says my sister to my mother in her quiet voice. My sister thinks because I cannot see that maybe I cannot hear very well, and she talks loud to me, and soft when she does not want me to hear, but I hear.

"You spilled," says my sister, loud.

"I can't be late," she says in her quiet voice to my mother. "Everybody's always late but me, and I won't be late."

My sister says she will take me to the park on her way to study. She gives me my jacket and tells me to wait for her outside on the steps.

I go down the outside steps. There are seven steps. Seven is my most magic number. Seven up, seven down, seven up, seven down. I go up and down, waiting for my sister.

My sister comes out. She takes my hand. She walks very fast, but I can still count the steps to the park, and I can still remember the turns. Someday I can go there by myself. I listen to the street noises and try to sort them out.

When we get to the park we go first to the bench. She waits to make sure I remember my way in the park. Fourteen steps to the bubbler. Around the bubbler, twenty steps to the curb.

I go back to the bench. I try to hurry, so my sister won't have to wait long and be cross. Now seventeen steps to the phone booth, four benches on the way, and I touch them all. Then I come back to the bench. My sister puts money in my pocket, so I can telephone.

She talks to me, and to herself.

"Filthy park," she says, and it is as if she were stepping on the words. "No grass. Trees in cages. Since when do benches and old newspapers make a park?" She pulls my jacket to straighten it.

Now she is gone and I have my morning in the sun.

I try each bench, but mine is still the best one.

I walk over to the telephone booth, touching the four benches on the way. I stand inside the booth. I feel to see whether there is any money in the telephone, but there is none. My sister says I should always check the telephone for money, but I have never found any.

I practice dialing our number, so I will be sure I have it right. Then I put my dime in and call. I let it ring two times, and then I hang up and get my dime back. My sister says, that way my mother will know I am all right.

I am sitting on my bench tapping my good luck song with my shoes when I hear the bells of an ice cream truck. I feel the money in my pocket. I have the dime, and I also have a bigger one. I know I have enough for an ice cream bar.

I walk out to the curb, touching the cages around the trees. I wait until the bells sound near, and I wave.

He stops. He is near enough for me to touch his cart. I hold out my money.

Now I feel him seeing me, but he does not take my money.

"Here," I say, but he does not take the money from me.

"Guess what?" he says, and his voice is soft and kind

as fur. "Every tenth kid wins a free ice cream bar, and you're the lucky one today."

I can feel him getting off his cart, and going around to open the place where he keeps his ice cream bars. I can feel him putting one near my hand, and I take it.

I start back to my bench.

"You gonna be okay by yourself now?" the ice cream man calls, so I know he is seeing me.

I sit on the bench. I listen for the sound of his cart starting up, and his bells ringing, but I can only hear the other sounds, the regular ones.

Then I hear him walking over to my bench.

I am sorry, because I only want to feel the ice cream, and see how long I can make it last. I do not want anyone to sit with me, but he is sitting with me now. I am afraid I will spill, and he will see me.

He starts to talk, and his voice is soft as a sweater.

His name is Abram. He tells me about the park.

My sister says the park is ugly and dirty.

Abram says there are a few little bits of paper, and a couple of cans and some bottles, but he says he can squint up his eyes and all those things lying around shine like flowers. Abram says you see what you want to see.

Part II

After I finish my ice cream bar, Abram gives me some paper clips so I can feel them in my pocket. He shows me how I can twist them to make little shapes.

After he leaves I feel them. There are seven paper clips.

The next day Abram brings me a balloon.

I can feel it round and tight. It tugs at the string.

Abram says, "Some balloons are filled with something special that makes them want to fly away, up to the sun, and this balloon is filled with that something special."

He says, "Some people are filled with something special that makes them pull and tug, too, trying to get up and away from where they are."

His voice is like a kitten curled on my shoulder.

He tells me my balloon is red, and then he tells me about colors.

He says, "Colors are just like sounds. Some colors are loud, and some colors are soft, and some are big and some are little, and some are sharp and some are tender, just like sounds, just like music."

What is the best color, I wonder?

He says, "All colors are the same, as far as that goes."

"There isn't a best color," says Abram. "There isn't a good color or a bad color. Colors are just on the outside. They aren't important at all. They're just covers for things, like a blanket. Color don't mean a thing," says Abram.

When my sister comes, she asks me where I got my balloon. I tell her about my friend.

I hold on to the string of my balloon while we walk.

We stop at a store. When we go in, I hold my balloon against me so it won't get hurt.

The store feels crowded. I hear a lady's voice. It sounds as if she was squeezing it out of her like the last bit of toothpaste in a tube.

The lady's voice says, "Better wait on this here colored lady first, so she can keep on going out of here and back where she belongs."

My sister takes my hand and pulls me away. I hold my balloon tight.

"So we're colored," says my sister to me as she pulls me along. "So what else is new? I've heard it a million times. I guess I heard it before I was born."

"Abram says color don't mean a thing," I say.

My sister drags me along, I can tell by her hand that she's mad.

"What does he know? Is he black, your friend?" she asks.

"I don't know," I say.

"You don't even know if your friend is black or not," says my sister.

"I wish everyone in the whole world was blind!" she cries.

When we get home, I tie the string of my balloon to my chair.

The next day when I am awake again, I cannot tell if it is morning, I hear noises but they are not the morning noises. My sister has her quiet voice, and I do not hear the little hard sounds of her heels making holes in the morning.

My sister is wearing slippers. She tells my mother she is not going to go to study today.

There is no hurry about today. I reach for my balloon. It does not float. It lies in my hand, tired and sad.

I lie there and listen to the sound of slippers on the kitchen floor.

I tap my good luck song against the wall over and over, but I hear the rain and know I will not go to the park today.

Tomorrow it will be a nice day. Tomorrow my sister will feel better, and I will go to the park and find Abram. He will make my balloon as good as new.

COLOR

What is the difference
Between one and another?
White as chalk,
White as snow,
Black as night,
Black as coal;

But people are pink
Or brown or tan
Or yellow-brown-pink
Or pinkish-brown-tan.

Not much difference, I think,
Between one and another.

By Eve Merriam

UNIT 3

BELONGING

Meg's First Day

BY DEBORAH KENT

I had practiced the walk to school three times the week before with Mom and my brother Sam, and the principal had even given me special permission to enter the building and learn where my classes would be held. Now, at the corner, I paused to review my directions: left on Prospect to the corner of Willow, across the street and left again down the long hill to Mulberry, across Mulberry, and half a block more to the signpost that marked the entrance to Ridge View High School. I used to envy Sam, his walks to school—friends ringing the doorbell, the group growing larger and noisier as it neared the school yard. From my bench on the front porch I would listen to them, running through the piles of dry leaves in the fall, throwing snowballs in the winter, teasing each other and making jokes about their teachers until their voices faded up the street.

The school bus was never like that. I would sit in the corner of my seat, reading a book or losing myself in daydreams, trying to draw away from the hubbub around me. No one had ever said so, but I was always sure that only weird kids had to take a bus and go to special school. The friends I made there never seemed as good as Sam's friends, who lived in the neighborhood, who could come over after school to play or do homework. There were voices ahead of me as I walked down the hill, the light, laughing voices of girls my own age.

"That's not what she told me," said the one on the right. "She told me he hung up on her."

"Yeah, but Sue, you can never believe what she says. She just likes to go after sympathy."

"I think she was telling the truth," said the one called Sue. Her voice was a little deeper and huskier than her friend's. "She was real upset, crying and all."

Suddenly I was afraid that they would turn and discover me behind them. Had they ever before seen someone who was blind? The rumble of traffic ahead told me that I was nearing Mulberry Street. I tried to tap my cane more lightly, left, right, left, right, assuring me of a clear path in front of me.

The girls had stopped, and I drew up beside them. "Paula's like that, though," Sue's friend said. "She can really put on a big act, and then . . ." However, her voice trailed off, and I felt them staring at me. My cane rang against the pavement. The tip dropped down to the street. I put out my foot and found the curb.

"Hi," I said into the silence.

A hand grasped my left wrist. "Careful," said Sue. "This is a real busy street."

"Are you going to school?" I asked as she propelled me forward.

"Yeah, are you?"

"Yes," I said, and I could think of nothing at all to add. What was Sue thinking, what was she wondering about me? If I could find the right words maybe I could put her at ease, maybe I could restore life to their conversation and it would go on where it had broken off, only now I would be part of it. I would find out about Paula and the boy who hung up on her. I would make them see that I was just another fifteen-year-old starting high school today — a little scared, but everybody was scared, and maybe we were all really worried about the same things.

"I can walk by myself," I said at the far curb, and pulled my arm free. For a few moments no one spoke, and my words echoed in my ears, too harsh, too resentful.

Still, when Sue's friend asked finally, "How are you going to manage?" I felt a flash of anger.

"Manage what?"

"Oh, you know — getting to classes, and what the teacher puts on the board — all that stuff."

I was explaining about visiting the school, about my Braille books, about being able to manage just fine, when Sue cried, "Darlene! Darlene, you nut, where've you been all summer?"

Then they were dashing ahead, melting into the laughing, chattering crowd that swarmed along the sidewalk. I felt like the only outsider as I pressed into the throng, alone and silent in the babble of greetings and gossip, clumsy and conspicuous with my white cane and my enormous book bag. I wished I had let Sam come with me after all.

I never found the signpost. As I searched for it through the crowd, my cane tangled among hurrying feet, and a boy exclaimed, "Why don't you watch where you're going?" But the signpost was quite unnecessary. I let the crowd sweep me around the turn, up the wall and through the heavy double front doors of Ridge View High School.

A week ago the corridor had stretched wide and empty, an avenue that lay so straight and clear I longed for a pair of roller skates. I could feel its height and width by the echoes my footsteps set bouncing from the walls and ceiling, and I walked a true course directly down the center. I had known that on this first morning it would not be the same, but nothing had prepared me for this frantic confusion. In the jostling crush of bodies I abandoned the use of my cane and fought ahead with one hand outstretched.

I don't know how I found the stairwell at the end of the hall. A bell rang, and feet thundered around me on the hollow treads. At least, I assured myself, no one had time to stare at me, to notice my uncertain steps and outstretched hand. At least for the moment I was no different from everyone else.

My homeroom, Two-Fourteen, was the third door on the right on the second-floor hall. A week ago I had found it easily by sliding my hand over the tall metal lockers and counting the doorways. But today I couldn't even reach the wall. I counted my steps and listened for clues, but my feet grew more and more unsure. At first I was afraid that I hadn't walked far enough, then that I had passed the door, and at last I seized a shoulder that brushed past me, and asked, "Where's Room Two-Four-teen?"

"This is Two-Twelve right here." It was a girl's voice, thin and nasal, with the hint of a whine.

"I must have passed it then." I turned back, so flustered that I forgot to thank her.

But she followed me protectively. "It must be this one," she said, grasping my arm just above the elbow. "Yeah, Two-Fourteen you wanted, right? This is it right here."

"Thanks," I said. I tried to free myself, to enter Two-Fourteen firmly on my own this first morning, but her fingers fastened more tightly and she pushed me ahead of her into the room. "I'm okay," I insisted, but she propelled me farther, and I was sure that the eyes of the entire class were fixed upon us.

"Here's a seat for you," she said. Her voice was loud in the relative quiet. "It's the first seat in the first row. That'll be easier for you." Her fingers relaxed their grip; she was gone.

Suddenly I realized that my book bag had grown very heavy. I set it down, folded my cane into its four short sections, and sank onto the hard plastic seat. My heart was pounding, and my hands were clammy with sweat.

All in all, it wouldn't have been a bad day if it hadn't been for the cafeteria. Students shouted and shoved, laughed and cursed. All of the regulations of Ridge View High were not enough to establish order there.

"Let me help you." It was a girl's voice, light and friendly. Gratitude overcame my desire for independence, and I was glad to let her maneuver me through the crowd. "Here's the end of the line," she said. "I've already got my tray, or I'd go through it with you. Can you make it from here?"

"Sure. Thanks."

Ahead of me two boys were deep in a discussion of the football team, and I followed them closely as the line crept forward. At last I heard the clatter of silverware just ahead. I found the stack of plastic trays, still hot and moist from recent washing, and hunted for the bins of knives and forks. "Come on! Move it!" a girl grumbled behind me. I grabbed a handful of silverware and slid my tray along the track.

"Hey," I said to the boy ahead of me, "can you tell me what there is here to eat?"

"All kinds of slop. You don't want any." His tray moved on and I followed, wondering miserably what I was passing up. The hiss of frying and the cloud of steam wafting from behind the counter told me we had reached the hot section. "Gimme some of that," the boy said, and I knew that I was next.

"What do you want?" the thin, cracked voice of an elderly woman demanded.

"I . . . I don't know. What is there?"

There was a moment of stunned silence before she burst out, "Oh, I'm so sorry, honey! I didn't realize! You like succotash? Let me give you some of this nice succotash. And how about some chicken croquettes? I'll give you a couple extra. I'm so sorry!"

But the worst part of all was still to come. At the cash register I realized that I still had to find a seat. The boys had dashed ahead, and I had lost their voices in the din. I thought of asking the girl behind me for help, but when I remembered her rough impatience, I was determined to go on alone. Hoisting my tray with one hand and wielding my cane with the other, I abandoned the safety of the line and entered the dining room.

"Is there an empty seat here?" I asked of anyone who might listen when my cane encountered a table leg.

"No," was the concise reply. Waxed paper rattled, a fork scraped a plate. I stood indecisively, taking in the sounds around me, trying to guess which way I should go. "There's a seat over there," a boy said finally.

"Over where?"

"Right over there. Over there on your left."

"Thanks," I made a sharp left turn and had taken two steps when the collision occurred. The tray leaped from my grasp, and I went down to shouts and the sound of shattering crockery. Inevitably someone cried, "Are you hurt?" and several demanded, "What happened?" Dazed and wretched, I sat on the floor amid the ruins of my lunch and my pride.

"Well," Dad asked at the dinner table, "how was your big day?"

"Fine," I said, and then, in case he might not believe me, "It was a little rough at first with so many kids."

"Did you get a lot of homework?" Sam wanted to know.

"Tons! I never got this much last year."

"Do you need me to read anything to you?" Mom asked.

"No, I'm okay. I even got started in study hall. Everything is working out fine," I paused, remembering the girls on the street. "I just wish everybody'd quit trying to be so darn helpful all the time."

"They don't know what you can do and what you can't do," Dad said. "You're going to have to educate them."

"But they really bug me, you know," I said. "I can

understand the kids maybe, but you'd think the teachers at least would be a little smarter."

"You'll just have to be patient," Mom said. As usual, she sided with Dad. "They've never known anyone before who was blind, and they're just trying to be nice."

"Nice!" I grumbled. Of course Dad and Mom were probably right, but that still didn't make it any easier. Only in the cafeteria, when I really did need someone, had no one offered assistance, and I had been too proud to ask. Maybe I was expecting people to read my mind.

"I've got the meanest math teacher," Sam said. "She's giving us twenty examples every night!"

"My history teacher's giving us a quiz every Friday," I said with a certain pride. "And in English we have to write a composition every week."

When dinner was over I followed Mom into the kitchen and started rinsing the plates. For a while we worked together in silence, putting the food away and loading the dishwasher. So I was caught off guard when she asked with sudden urgency, "How do you really feel about school?"

"I'm glad I'm there," I said. There was a lot I wasn't telling her, but that much, at least, was true.

The TEST

by Phil Aponte

I was new in the neighborhood. We had just moved, and I didn't like it. I had to start all over again making new friends. Days passed, and still I had no friends.

Then one night a guy talked to me. His name was Ron, and he was about a year ahead of me in school. "We have a little gang around here," he said, "and if you're not afraid, we might let you in."

I said, "What do you mean?"

"Be here tomorrow night," he said, "and you'll find out."

Ron and three other guys found me on the street the next night. I wasn't scared, but I thought maybe I had made a mistake. I had never been in trouble. Now I didn't like Ron's looks, and I didn't like the looks of the other three guys, either.

Then Ron said, "Well, Phil, are you ready for your test?"

"Okay, Ron," I said, "but I don't want to get into any trouble."

"Don't worry," he said. "The police won't bother us."

We walked until we got to an empty building across the street from where I lived. "Let's go up, Phil," he said, pushing open the front door.

I looked into the dark hall and said, "Where are we going?"

"To the roof," he said, "if you're not chicken."

Ron, another guy, and I went up the stairs — first, second, third, top floor, and then out on the roof.

"Wait a minute," he said. I saw that the next building was about seven feet away, and that two of the boys were over there on the roof. I walked to the edge, looked over, and leaped back! The street was a long way down, and there was nothing between the two buildings.

He said, "You aren't getting worried, are you, Phil?"

"No," I said, trying to sound brave. "Let's get on with this test."

Ron smiled, and we watched the boys on the other roof lift a thick iron pipe that seemed to be over seven feet long. When they laid the pipe from roof to roof, I turned to Ron and asked, "What's that for?"

"You're going to swing on a bar and show us how strong you are," he said.

I looked and saw that the door to the roof was still

open. "Well, it's time for me to leave Ron and his friends," I thought.

Then Ron said, "You have to take the test, Phil. If you try to run away, you might slip and fall over, or you might run into one of us and get pushed over."

I grabbed the end of the bar. The two guys on the other roof were holding the other end. I put out a foot and looked down. Then I grabbed for dear life and put out my other foot. I was on my way, hand over hand. My feet kicked out into space. I had a little more to go, but my hands were sweating, and my arms were starting to hurt. Then I made it! I put my foot up onto the roof, and one of the boys pushed it off. "Sorry," he said, "you're not welcome on this side."

I tried once more to climb up, and again he pushed my foot off. I started back, and about halfway there, I couldn't go on. I couldn't feel my hands any more.

"Please let me go," I said. I wasn't one of them, and I guess I had known it from the beginning.

The boys laughed and Ron said, "We'll see you around, Phil." Then he and the others started to leave.

"No, Ron!" I called. "If you go, I'll never get away from here!"

"Look, Phil, if you get out of this, you're one of the boys," he said, "and if you don't, well, you can be sure we'll be at your funeral." Then he and the others left. They did not even look back.

For a long time, I didn't move. The bar might come off the two roofs, because there was no one to hold it now.

Again I inched up to the building, and the bar started slipping. I reached for the edge of the building, and grabbed it. Then the bar fell! My arms were high

over my head, and my body was close against the building. I lifted myself, slowly swinging one foot onto the
building. With one last pull, I rolled onto the roof. I lay
there, my eyes closed. My arms and legs were dead to
the world.

After a while, I got up and went home.

My mother asked, "Where have you been?"

"Out on the street," I said, wondering if she knew
about the test.

I remember
wanting to be big like Mikey,
to stand around looking cool.
Now that I am,
it's OK I guess.
Some days I won't even smile
no matter what.
That's part of being cool.
The only thing is
I can't cry if I want to.

Nikki Grimes

UNIT 4

FREEDOM FIGHTERS

Sojourner Truth's Freedom Ride

by Helen Stone Peterson

Sojourner Truth was a slave until she was twenty-nine years old. After the Civil War she came to Washington to help black people who were now free but very poor. This story tells what happened to her in Washington. After she became free, she would help other slaves become free.

The War Department asked Sojourner to work in Freedmen's Hospital in Washington. It was crowded with black men who had been wounded in the war. There was a serious shortage of nurses.

"I shall be glad to do all I can," Sojourner told the officials. She began her new work at once.

One morning she started for the hospital carrying a heavy sack of fruit. Suddenly she decided to take a streetcar.

When she first arrived in Washington, the horse-drawn streetcars were segregated. Special cars carried signs, saying "Colored Persons May Ride in This Car." Now the signs were gone. A law had been passed to forbid segregation on the streetcars. Blacks were shy, however, about claiming their right to ride in any streetcar they wanted.

Sojourner waved at a streetcar to stop. It went right by. Another streetcar came along, but the conductor paid no attention to Sojourner's signal. "I want to ride!" she screamed. "I want to ride! I want to ride!"

Drivers stopped their carriages and their wagons to see what the cause of this excitement was. A traffic jam built up, forcing the streetcar to stop. Sojourner jumped in and took a seat.

The conductor glared at her. "Get outside and sit on the platform with the driver."

"I shall not," said Sojourner fearlessly. "I have paid

five cents' fare, same as these other people. I intend to keep my seat."

"Do as I tell you or I'll throw you out!" roared the conductor.

"You better not try that, or I'll have the law on you," warned Sojourner. "I know my rights and you can't trample on them." The conductor turned away.

Sojourner was delighted with her victory. Later, walking up the path to the hospital, she promised herself, "I shall keep riding. Before I'm through, the conductors will change their ways."

A few days after that, Sojourner had to cross the city on an errand for the hospital. She waved at a streetcar, but it kept going. She ran after it as fast as she could. When the streetcar stopped to take on some white passengers, Sojourner leaped aboard.

She gasped, "It's a shame to make a lady run so."

The conductor said angrily, "I have a notion to throw you off."

Sojourner refused to back down. "If you try that, it will cost you more than your car and horses are worth," she cried. The conductor let her stay.

Several weeks later Sojourner battled again with the conductors. She and a white friend, Laura Haviland, had put in a hard day collecting supplies for the wounded black soldiers. Loaded with packages, they started for the hospital. Mrs. Haviland signaled a streetcar, and it stopped. Sojourner climbed quickly into the car.

"Get out of the way and let this lady come in," yelled the conductor.

"I am a lady too," said Sojourner.

He said no more. Soon Sojourner and Mrs. Haviland had to change to another streetcar. As they stepped in, a white passenger objected.

"Get off!" the conductor ordered harshly.

"I shall not," Sojourner answered. The conductor grabbed her shoulder.

"Don't put her out," said Mrs. Haviland.

The conductor asked angrily, "Does she belong to you?"

"No," replied Mrs. Haviland calmly. "She belongs to humanity."

"Then take her and go!" shouted the conductor. He slammed Sojourner against the door, but she refused to leave.

By the time she reached the hospital, she was in great pain. Physicians found that her shoulder had been badly hurt. Sojourner went to the police, and the conductor was arrested. He lost his job.

After that, conductors in Washington changed their ways. They stopped the streetcars to take on black people who wanted to ride.

ROSA PARKS
by Eloise Greenfield

Rosa Parks was a seamstress living in Montgomery, Alabama, in 1955. At that time black and white people were segregated on buses and in other public places. This story tells how Rosa Parks' actions helped rid the South of "Jim Crow" laws.

PART I — DON'T RIDE THE BUS

On Thursday evening, December 1, 1955, Rosa left work and started home. She was tired. Her shoulders ached from bending over the sewing machine all day. "Today, I'll ride the bus," she thought.

She got on and sat in the first seat for blacks, right behind the white section. After a few stops the seats were filled. A white man got on. He looked for an empty seat. Then he looked at the driver. The driver came over to Rosa.

"You have to get up," he said.

All of a sudden Rosa knew she was not going to give up her seat. It was not fair. She had paid her money just as the man had. This time she was not going to move.

"No," she said softly.

"You'd better get up, or I'll call the police," the driver said.

It was very quiet on the bus now. Everyone stopped talking and watched. Still, Rosa did not move.

"Are you going to get up?"

"No," she repeated.

The driver left the bus and returned with two policemen.

"You're under arrest," they told her.

Rosa walked off the bus. The policemen put her in their car and drove to the police station. One policeman stuck a camera in her face and took her picture. Another took her fingerprints. Then she was locked in a cell.

Rosa felt very bad, sitting in that little room with iron bars. But she did not cry. She was a religious woman, and she thought of her faith in God. She said a silent prayer. Then she waited.

Someone who had seen Rosa arrested called Edgar Daniel Nixon of the NAACP. Mr. Nixon went right away to the police station and posted a hundred-dollar bond for Rosa. This meant that she could leave, but that she promised to go to court on Monday for her trial.

Rosa left the police station. She had been locked up for two and a half hours. Mr. Nixon drove her home. At her apartment Rosa, her husband, Mr. Nixon, and Fred Gray, a lawyer, talked about what had happened. They thought they saw a way to solve the problem of the buses.

Mr. Gray would go into court with Rosa. He would

prove that the bus company was not obeying the United States Constitution. The Constitution is an important paper that was written by the men who started the United States. It says that all citizens of the United States must be treated fairly.

The next morning Rosa went to her job as usual. Her employer was surprised to see her. He had read about her arrest in the newspaper, and he thought she would be too upset to come in. Some of the white workers gave Rosa mean looks and would not speak to her. But she went on with her work.

That night Rosa met with a group of ministers and other black leaders of the city. Dr. Martin Luther King was one of the ministers. The black men and women of Montgomery were angry.

"If the bus company won't treat us courteously," one leader said, "we won't spend our money to ride the buses. We'll walk!"

After the meeting some of the people printed little sheets of paper. These sheets of paper, called leaflets, said, "DON'T RIDE THE BUS TO WORK, TO TOWN, TO SCHOOL, OR ANYWHERE, MONDAY, DECEMBER 5." They also invited people to a church meeting on Monday night. The leaflets were left everywhere — in mail boxes, on porches, in drugstores.

On Sunday morning black ministers all over the city preached about Rosa in their churches. Dr. King preached from his pulpit at the Dexter Avenue Baptist Church.

The preachers said, "Brothers and sisters, if you don't like what happened to Rosa Parks and what has been happening to us all these years, do something about it. Walk!"

Near-empty bus rides through Montgomery. Blacks made up 70% of the population.

And people said, "Amen. We'll walk."

On Monday morning, no one was riding the buses. There were many people on the streets, but everyone was walking. They were cheering because the buses were empty.

Rosa got up early that morning. She went to court with her lawyer for her trial. The judge found her guilty. But she and her lawyer did not agree with him. Her lawyer said, "We'll get a higher court to decide. If we have to, we'll take the case to the highest court in the United States."

Mrs. Rosa Parks was escorted up the Montgomery County courthouse steps on March 19 by E. D. Nixon, former president of the Alabama NAACP.

That night thousands of people went to the church meeting. There were so many people that most of them had to stand outside and listen through a loudspeaker.

First there was prayer. Then Rosa Parks was introduced. She stood up slowly. The audience rose to its feet and clapped and cheered. After Rosa sat down, several ministers gave their speeches. Finally Dr. Martin Luther King started to speak.

"We are tired," he said.

"Yes, Lord," the crowd answered.

"We are tired of being kicked around," he said.

"Yes, Lord," they answered.

"We're not going to be kicked around anymore," Dr. King said. "We walked one day. Now we are going to have a real protest. We are going to keep walking until the bus company gives us fair treatment."

After Dr. King finished speaking, the Montgomery Improvement Association was formed to plan the protest. Dr. King was made president.

Then there was hymn singing and hand clapping. The people went home feeling good. All that walking was not going to be easy, but they knew they could do it.

PART II — FREEDOM WALKS

The Montgomery Improvement Association and the churches bought as many cars and station wagons as they could afford. There were telephone numbers that people could call when they needed a ride. Housewives answered the phones. Rosa was one of them. Her employer had told her that she was no longer needed. When someone called for a ride, Rosa would tell the drivers where to go. But there were not nearly enough cars.

Old people and young people walked. The children walked a long way to school. The men and women walked to work, to church, everywhere. In the morning it was like a parade. People were going to work, some riding on the backs of mules, some riding in wagons pulled by horses, but most of them walking. Sometimes they sang.

In the evening the parade went the other way, people going home. The newspapers called Montgomery "the walking city."

It was hard. Many people had to leave home long before daylight to get to work on time. They got home late at night. Their feet hurt. But they would not give up. The bus company kept saying it would not change. And black people kept on walking.

The enemies of the blacks tried to frighten them. They threw bottles at the walkers. Some homes were bombed.

One day Rosa's phone rang. She picked it up.

"Hello," she said.

"You're the cause of all this trouble," a voice said. "You should be killed."

Rosa hung up. The calls kept coming, day after day. Rosa was afraid, but she knew she could not stop.

After two months, more than a hundred leaders of

The black citizens of Montgomery walked all year.

the protest were arrested. Rosa was among them. A court had said that the protest was against the law. The leaders posted bond, and went right back to their work.

Reporters came to Montgomery from all over the United States and from other countries. They wrote stories in their newspapers about the arrests.

Rosa began to travel to other cities, making speeches. She told about the hardships of the people. Many of the people she spoke to helped. They gave her money to pay for bonds and to buy gas for the cars.

The black citizens of Montgomery walked all winter, all spring, all summer and fall in all kinds of weather. The bus company lost thousands of dollars.

In November, the Supreme Court, the highest court in the United States, said that the bus company had to change. It had not been obeying the Constitution.

That night the Ku Klux Klan paraded past the homes of the blacks. The people stood in their doorways and watched. They were no longer afraid. They had won.

Several weeks later, the bus company obeyed the Supreme Court and changed its rules. A year had passed since Rosa refused to give up her seat. Now blacks could sit in any seat. They would not have to get up for anyone.

Black people in other places read about Montgomery. They began to work for fair treatment of blacks in their own cities.

They said, "If Rosa Parks had the courage to do this, we can do it too." They called her "the Mother of the Civil Rights Movement."

One day a group of reporters went to Rosa's home. They took her to ride on the bus. She entered through the front door. For the first time she sat anywhere she chose. And she would stay there until the end of her ride.

No one could ever ask her to get up again.

HARRIET TUBMAN

by Johanna Johnston

The woods were dark all around her.
There was no road, no path,
no trail.
She could only tell what direction she was going
by looking up at the stars and following the
bright one that hung low
in the north.
When clouds covered the sky so that it was dark too,
she had to feel her way. She
put out her hands and felt the tree trunks.
Moss grew on the northern side of tree trunks.
She felt for the moss, and where it grew it
showed her the way.

When day came, she had to hide
in bushes or behind rocks. When there were storms
she had nothing but bushes or trees
to cover her.
After a while, she had no more food.
Sometimes she found berries. And she drank
from brooks.
On and on she went, night after night,
covering mile after mile.
Sometimes, not often, she came near a house
where she thought there were people who
would help her.
She would go to the house when it was day,
and the people would hide her for a day
while she ate something and rested.

Then when night came, she would
start on again.

At last, after many nights and days,
Harriet Tubman knew she was out of the South,
where she had been a slave.
She was in the North where Blacks could be free.
Soon she was in the city of Philadelphia
where there were white men and women who
would help her.
She made her way to those people and they
welcomed her with joy.
Harriet Tubman was safe and free.
"Now you must rest," they told her.
"After that, we will find you a place to live
and a job so that you can have a good life."

Harriet said, "Thank you. Yes I want a job
for a while. But as soon as I have earned
a little money, I must go back down South again."
"Go South again?" said her friends.
They were horrified.
"How can you think of making that terrible journey
again?"
Harriet said, "I have brothers there, and
my mother and father. I have friends — all of them
still in slavery. Now that I know the way
I must go back and lead them to freedom also."
Her friends said, "You can't bring so many.
You will be caught."
Harriet said, "I will just have to make many trips."
Nobody could make her change her mind.
Before many weeks had passed, she was on her way.

IDA B. WELLS

by Eve Merriam

Holly Springs in Mississippi was a pretty little place
with Spanish moss growing as soft as lace,
with glossy magnolias with songbirds in trees,
with juleps and jasmine in the sweet evening breeze,
with dusty back roads and garden-front streets,
with parasols and fans and the Klan in sheets.

With one season's gain and another's losses
and some nights lit up by fiery crosses,
Holly Springs was the picture of a pleasant Southern town,
and Ida B. was born there beautiful and brown.

      Sweet as a blossom
      on a peach tree,
      there she was —
      lovely
      for all to see.

      It was a pleasure
      to watch her go by
      with her delicate figure
      and sudden smile,
      and always dressed
      in the daintiest style;
      Ida B., Ida B.,
      so graceful to see
      with her diamond-bright eyes
      and soft hair piled high.

But something was wrong
with sweet Ida B.
There it was
plain
for all to see
and it was a worry

to watch her go by:
>   that girl looked everyone straight in the eye.
>   That girl didn't mumble, she opened her mouth:
>   didn't she know that the South was the South?

>   Young Ida B.,
>   beware,
>   beware,
>   trouble
>   will come
>   if
>   you
>   don't
>   have
>   a
>   care!

Ida B. took trouble in her stride.
Only fourteen when both parents died.
Four younger brothers and sisters to tend,
homework and housework and cook clean and mend:
It looked like a long road that never would bend . . .
But Ida B. managed to provide.

She finished with school
and started to teach,
but kept reaching out
for
what wasn't in reach.

>   Ida B.,
>   Ida B.,
>   bound
>   to
>   declare, reach.

more trouble
will come
if
you
don't
have
a
care!

Why can't you lock up the thoughts in your heart?
Must you always speak out just the way that you feel?
When will you learn that
real
and
ideal
(like the two races)
are far apart?

Ida B.,
Ida B.,
please have a care;
trouble's just looking for someone to share —
you'll be
that someone,
now
be
aware!

Ida B. moved
from the small 'Sippi town
and everyone hoped that
she'd soon settle down

Memphis was bigger
than Holly Springs,

and yet she found there
the very same things.
The streets and the sidewalks
were smooth and wide,
but a Black still had to step aside.
The mockingbirds sang
as back home they'd sung,
and sometimes from lamp posts
dark shadows were flung
just as magnolias
had heavily hung
when some special weight
on the branches
swung . . .

Ida B. couldn't learn
to hold her tongue.

> Ida B.,
> Ida B.,
> won't you take care?
> Can't you accept
> that life is unfair?
> Besides,
> it's a stranger,
> you don't know the man.
> Go home and prepare
> tomorrow's lesson plan.
> *You're* getting by,
> why look around?
> Trouble's just aching
> to be found.

But Ida B. walked with her head held high,
and persisted in staring life straight in the eye.

The subjects she taught seemed less vital each day.
She was earning more in Memphis on her teacher's pay;
Each month she put a part of it away.
Saved and saved
for what she craved . . .

    . . . now do you suppose
    she wanted a castle
    or carriage
    or clothes?
    To be bowed to,
    kowtowed to,
    satined and velveted,
    silkened and plushed?

    You know her by now:
    it was not to be hushed
Ida B. had a dream and she scrimped for the day:
if she owned a newspaper,
she'd have her own way;
then none could blue-pencil,
she'd speak her own say!

By the age of only twenty-three,
the dream of Ida B.
became reality.

Now she could teach what she wanted to teach
in her weekly paper:
the *Memphis Free Speech*,

for she was the editor
(the co-owner, too)
and could print all the news
from her own point of view.

Wasn't it shockingly long past time
for lynching to be counted a major crime?
Mobs went unpunished for their attacks.
— Because the victims were usually blacks?
— Was that why the guilty kept getting off free?
Dangerous questions from Ida B.

      Dear Ida B.,
      please don't crusade;
      why can't you be
      just a little afraid?
      If you have to protest,
      write of things far away.
      Don't interfere
      with what's
      here
      every day!

      Condemn the tyrants of ancient Rome
      (don't mention the sheriffs so close to home.)
      Indict abstract evils with your pen —
      and not our local businessmen.

Ida B. was human —
of course she was scared.
But being Ida B.,
the truth wasn't spared.

Three young Black men were lynched one night.
It was clear enough, there was plenty of light
to see the faces of violence and hate.
Ida B. didn't stop to hesitate.

She did what she knew was bound to enrage.
She went and named names on her paper's front page.

Not only the names of the red-necked mob,
but the "gentlemen" who had incited the "job" —
the men of means
behind the scenes
who were whitely polite
and oh so nice
and quiet as ice.
— And who didn't like the competition
of Blacks aspiring to *their* position.

> Ida B., Ida B.,
> too late to beware;
> now trouble's lunging from everywhere!
> Hear the howling voices?
> The stamping feet?
> They're coming closer —
> they're right on your street!
> The torches are blazing!
> They're up the stair!

They burned down her office.
Smashed the press.
And they'd have got to
Ida B. unless —

— friends came to rescue her just in time.
Or there'd have been one more lynching crime.

Ida B.,
Ida B.,
Ida begone,
flee
before
the
bloody
dawn.

She couldn't go back to Tennessee,
but she kept on being Ida B.

Up North in Illinois, in Lincoln's own state
the number of lynchings still was great.
No one knew how many each year
were murdered by mobs in hysterical fear.
No one had ever kept records before.
Ida B. tallied up the terrible score.

And rather than praying to change some natures
she campaigned for Blacks in legislatures.
Instead of kindly sympathy,
she believed in action,
did Ida B.
It was good to have faith in a worthy cause,
but better to pass — and enforce — the laws.

She became a crusading editor's wife,
and went on enjoying the rest of her life:

organized women in clubs, and lectured to youth,
and kept agitating
to print the truth.
Stayed pretty as ever,
with her head held high
and kept on looking
life
straight
in
the
eye.

Clearly outspoken
with head held high
and always looking life straight in the eye.

UNIT 5

FAMOUS FIRSTS

Elizabeth Blackwell

By Jean Lee Latham

In 1845, when Elizabeth Blackwell was 24 years old, she decided that she wanted to be a doctor. She could not get pre-medical training in a college, because she was a woman. Two doctors helped her. They let her study in their office. But no medical college had ever allowed a woman to study medicine.

Elizabeth wrote to every big medical school in America. They all said no! She got catalogs from all the smaller colleges. With friendly Dr. Elder's help, Elizabeth wrote to twelve of them. One by one they said no!

October came. There was no time to lose. Medical schools were opening. Elizabeth was 26. For almost two years she had studied night and day to prepare for medical school.

Finally a letter came from Geneva Medical College in western New York State. The faculty had let the student body vote on whether or not they should admit a woman. The students had voted yes! They would welcome Miss Elizabeth Blackwell!

She would be starting late, but at last she could begin! She smiled to herself all the way to Geneva.

Elizabeth got a room in a hotel when she arrived, then went out to find a boardinghouse.

Three landladies said, "No rooms!"

"But you have a sign out!" Elizabeth said to the third one.

"Not for the kind of woman who'd be a doctor!"

She stayed in the hotel overnight. The next day she started to hunt again for a boardinghouse.

At last a Miss Waller took her in.

"I don't know how you'll get along in that college," she said. "The boys are so rowdy that some people want to close the school."

MEDICAL SCHOOL

FOR MEN ONLY

"I'm sure I'll get along," Elizabeth said. "I have four younger brothers."

She moved into her room. Then she went to the college. The boys stared at her and whispered to each other. What was wrong?

The faculty seemed stiff and uneasy. The professor of anatomy was away. His assistant would not let Elizabeth in the class. She had never felt so unwelcome in her life.

It was a long time before she learned the truth. The faculty had not wanted to admit her. They thought they could dodge the problem by letting the students vote on it. So the faculty had said the vote must be unanimous, without a single no. Those boys never agreed about anything!

But the boys had thought it was a joke. Maybe some other school was playing a trick on them. So they voted to admit her. The faculty had to go along with that vote.

Then Dr. Webster, the professor of anatomy, arrived. He greeted her with smiles. After that, the mood of the students changed.

After two days Dr. Webster said, "My dear Miss Blackwell, you are a lion tamer! Our boys have been so rowdy that you could hardly hear yourself talk. Now they are behaving like perfect gentlemen."

But the people in the boardinghouse still did not speak to her. The women of the town stared and whispered. Elizabeth heard the gossip. She was "either mad or bad." Only a crazy woman, or a wicked one, would try to be a doctor!

Elizabeth had never been so alone in her life. She went to school, sat in classes, and took notes. She walked out, keeping her eyes straight ahead. The boys were friendly enough in class, but she never saw them outside the college.

An Outrageous Idea

BY FLORENCE MEIMAN WHITE

"SUFFRAGE IS ONLY THE FIRST STEP TOWARD WOMEN'S EQUALITY, ladies, and most women in our country still do not enjoy this basic right. There is more, much more to be done."

Jeannette was addressing the women sitting in her parlor in Missoula. Two years before they had worked with her to bring suffrage to the women of Montana. They ranged in age from twenty to sixty, and in dress from elegant city fashions to simple country clothes. But they were united by one great passion — the freedom and welfare of women.

As Jeannette paused, the women nodded and murmured, "We must indeed have women in government. Women can govern as well as men. Of course we agree with you."

When the room was quiet, Jeannette continued in a low voice. "I want to run for the Congress of the United States." This was the first announcement of her plans. She had discussed the matter only with her brother, Wellington.

For a moment, there was dead silence, then a babel of voices, amazed and unbelieving.

"Why, Jeannette, there's never been a woman in Congress."

"You'll never be elected."

"Why don't you run for a lower office?"

"Yes. Start in the State Assembly. We'll work for you there."

For another hour, questions, answers, arguments filled the room. Jeannette tried to still their doubts. She closed with her most convincing argument.

"Ladies, there must be a woman in Congress. Only a woman will work for the right of all American women

Jeannette Rankin, about the time she was running for her first term in Congress

EMBERS/CIBC

to vote. Only a woman will work for an amendment to the United States Constitution giving women that right. Just being there will make it harder for a man to vote against such an amendment."

The women knew Jeannette's ability. But much as they admired and respected her, they would not endorse a woman for one of the highest offices in the land. The idea was outrageous.

After the women left, Jeannette remained seated, her fingers braided together in her lap. She had hoped, she had tried, but the women were not ready. They had not come as far as she had in their thinking. Without their help, could she convince the citizens of Montana to elect her to the Congress of the United States?

Deep in thought, Jeannette had not noticed that the sun had set and the room was getting dark. She rose from her chair, pushed back the soft brown hair from her face, and lit the lamps. Tomorrow morning she would go to see her brother, give him a report and hear what he had learned. Wellington had offered to find out what some of the political leaders thought about a woman in Congress. She dared to hope that he would have better news than she had.

Next day she sat in her brother's sunny law office in Helena, the capital of Montana, and told him about the meeting. "They were shocked at the idea. Called it outrageous." Her voice was gloomy.

Wellington's voice was just a little less gloomy. "So were the people I spoke with. 'Keep your sister from making a fool of herself,' they advised."

Both were silent for a few moments. Jeannette broke the silence. "What do you think, Wellington?" She knew she would get an honest answer from her brother.

Wellington folded his arms on his large mahogany desk and leaned toward his sister. "You can do it, Jeannette. Your work for the suffrage movement made you the best known woman in Montana. You can get the nomination, and you can win the election." His voice was sure.

Jeannette was cheerful as she rose to leave. "Thanks, Wellington. Thanks." She kissed him on the cheek. "If I run, will you be my campaign manager?" she asked hesitantly. "You bet I will, and I'll get you elected," he promised. They both laughed as he walked with her to the door.

While driving home, Jeannette thought about Wellington's advice. He had not only urged her to run, he had offered to pay for her campaign. But without the help of those capable women. . . . For the next few months, she was busy talking to political leaders to learn how much support she could get.

In less than two years after Montana women had gained the right to vote, one of them was running for one of the highest offices in the country. Even more astonishing — for the first time in the history of the United States a woman was running for Congress.

As soon as Jeannette announced her candidacy, the women who had doubted her came to her support as they had done before. She would be running against three men. She was young, intelligent, attractive. Could she beat them?

The Rankin family came out in full force to work in her campaign. Wellington was her manager as he had promised. Her sisters, Harriet, Mary, Grace and Edna spoke to the voters. The women who had worked with her for woman suffrage did the same. They traveled all

Jeannette Rankin and her brother Wellington in front of the family home in Missoula, **Montana**

over the state. Montana was large, the roads rough, the mountains rugged.

Jeannette spoke to the women: "I will work for child labor laws to protect your children and for education laws to educate them. I will work for an eight-hour work day for women and for the same rights to jobs and education as men have. And I will work for a suffrage amendment to the Constitution of our country so that all American women will have the right to vote."

To the workingmen she said: "I will work for safe and sanitary working conditions in mines, forests, factories, wherever people work."

And to the mothers and fathers of Montana who were frightened by a European war, she made a solemn promise: "I will do everything in my power to keep our country out of war and your sons safe at home."

Jeannette now had to fight against enemies — the mine owners, the liquor interests, and the rich women who did not believe in rights for all women. They sent people out to talk against "that woman who wants to be in Congress." "A woman's place is in the house," said one speaker. Jeannette's answer was, "Yes, in the House of Representatives." "Politics is a dirty business," said another. "Women don't belong in it." Jeannette quickly retorted, "Who made it dirty?"

Jeannette's popularity grew. The people believed her. Her good sense and sincerity appealed to the working men and women of Montana. "She'll work for us down there in Washington," they told their neighbors.

On Election Day, Jeannette's friends called everyone who had a telephone. "Good morning. Have you voted for Jeannette Rankin?" they asked in a cheery voice.

In spite of her strong spirit, the next few days were difficult ones for Jeannette. There were no counting machines, and votes had to be counted by hand. Meanwhile reports had her losing, then winning, and with them went Jeannette's hopes.

At last the final count came in. Headlines blazed the result in the newspapers all over the world:

FIRST WOMAN ELECTED TO THE CONGRESS OF THE UNITED STATES!

Respect

by Angel Nieto

We are all different
and i respect that
as i respect your right to be
and i respect your right to become
as i respect your right to love
and i respect your right to fight
but don't expect respect from me
if you don't love if you don't fight
if you are . . . if you become . . .
indifferent.

UNIT 6

SCHOOL DAYS

Cristina's Diary

by Esther De Michael Cervantes and Alex Cervantes

Dear Diary,

Today was Angie's baby brother's birthday. I went to his party. His American name is George but his Chinese name is Ging Ging. George doesn't talk very much. I think it's because he's shy. Of course he's only four years old. One of the funniest things George did was to put his finger in the cake when Mr. Tang was taking a picture. Everyone laughed. But Mrs. Tang didn't think it was funny. She got embarrassed.

Angie has other relatives from China. Even though they have been in the United States for a long time and speak English very well, they like to speak Chinese with each other. That's the way the Mexican people feel. We speak English at school because most of the teachers want us to, but at home we speak our own language. A lot of teachers at our school get real mad when we speak Spanish. They say we're in America, and so we should only speak English. But my Father says that the Mexicans were here long before the Anglos, and so the Anglos should learn Spanish.

When I was in second grade my Father got in an argument with Mrs. Olson about speaking Spanish. I used to speak Spanish a lot when I was younger so sometimes I forgot to use English at school. My teacher, Mrs. Olson, told me never to use Spanish in her room again. My Father got angry. He went down to school and had a long talk with the principal. After that Mrs. Olson never told me anything any more but she still told the other kids "in English, in English!" when they used Spanish.

Last year Mrs. Huerta became our principal. She wants the teachers to learn Spanish so they can help the children more, because most of the kids at our school speak Spanish and can read in Spanish also. Mrs. Huerta

also wants some teachers to learn Chinese to help those kids, too.

I used to think it was strange to have two names like George. I would feel funny. Who would I be? Cristina Carlota Aguilar or Christine Charlotte Adams? But then again maybe it would be a good idea, because the teachers pronounce the Mexican names all wrong anyway. Like Jaime's name, for instance. Sometimes they call him "James" and sometimes they call him "Jayme." Jaime knows they're talking to him but he refuses to answer. The teachers call him "defiant" and "stubborn," but Jaime says they wouldn't like it if he pronounced *their* names wrong. Mrs. Olson used to call me Christine. I always wondered why she called me that. Everyone else called me Tina or Cristina, but Mrs. Olson must have been hard of hearing or something because she always called me Christine or, worse yet, Chris. I *hate* to be called Chris.

Good night

Cristina

Dear Diary,

Mr. Torres is absent again. We got another substitute. She seemed nice. "My name is Ms. Riles. Your teacher will be back tomorrow. He misses all of you very much. My Spanish isn't the best, so please help me out when I get stuck. I'll be using mostly English. Maybe one of you would like to translate when someone doesn't understand. Mr. Torres said I could do something different with you today. I brought my bag of tricks. It should be a fun day. I hope you learn something, too." She was okay, but we all missed Mr. Torres. I think that if I was a teacher like Mr. Torres and smart like him, I wouldn't stay in this neighborhood. I asked him why he stays and he says he likes to see kids learn. "But aren't there kids everywhere? Couldn't you teach somewhere else?" I asked.

"I like helping the kids who live here, and I'm liking this school more now," he explained. "We've begun a program where the kids can speak Spanish and that will help them learn faster. Then they will have more *opportunities* when they grow up. I grew up here, so I understand the kids more than a lot of other teachers. If I made it, I know other kids can make it. It's going to be better in Los Angeles when you grow up. We'll make it better. You'll see."

I hope Mr. Torres is right.

So long

Dear Diary,

Today was the last day of school. It was a happy-sad day. Mr. Torres gave us a party, of course, and prizes — books, jacks, puzzles, stuff like that. He said we were the best class he has ever had. "In fact," he said, smiling at us, "you've been so great that I'm going to be a sixth grade teacher next year. Mrs. Huerta said I can keep my class if I like. And that's what I'm going to do."

Everyone started shouting "YEAAAA!" Ronald and Jaime were clapping real hard and Angie started jumping up and down. After we settled down, Donna Marie and Rosabelia brought in our surprise to Mr. Torres. We had hidden it in the coat closet. It was a big cake that Jaime's father had baked. The blue letters on the frosting said, "To Mr. Torres, World's Best Teacher." Then we gave him a bunch of presents. He got ties, men's cologne, books, handkerchiefs, and a pen. Angie and I bought him a new Hans Christian Andersen book (like mine) because his old one was falling apart. The new one was larger and nicer than the old one.

Then Ángel gave him a big card. Ángel had done the art work and Angie and I wrote the words. On the front of the card is a picture of a reporter. The words are, "I snooped around for the best news yet and here's the scoop."

And on the inside was a drawing of Mr. Torres and the words said:

To Mr. Torres,
> You're the front page banner
> > and the best top story,
> You're the number 1 photo
> > and the scoop of the year,
> And we were lucky
> > to be taught by you!

All the kids had signed the card. Angie wrote, "To the bestest and nicest teacher I'll ever have." And I wrote, "To the only teacher I've ever liked."

Mr. Torres said, "You're great. Every one of you."

When it came time to say good-bye, Mr. Torres told us to have fun during the summer. "And don't forget the library. Read a lot of books," he said.

We promised we would. Then he walked us to the gate. All the children kissed or hugged him.

Angie and I kept waving to him until we got to the bottom of the hill. Then we turned the corner. "This will be our best summer," Angie said. "And next year's going to be even better than this year was."

"I know. I can hardly wait!" I said.

'Til then, Diary,

Tina

Roll of Thunder, Hear My Cry

by Mildred B. Taylor

These stories are chapters in a book called *Roll of Thunder, Hear My Cry* by Mildred Taylor. After you read "Hand-Me-Down Books" and "An Unwelcome Visit," perhaps you will want to read all of *Roll of Thunder*.

The first story takes place in Mississippi in 1933. It is the first day of a new term. Cassie and Little Man are sister and brother. They are in the same class in school. The teacher gave out books for the new year. The books are old and soiled. Little Man is very disappointed, because he had wanted a new book for the new term. He tried to return the book to the teacher and exchange it for a newer one. The teacher became very angry and sent him back to his seat.

HAND-ME-DOWN BOOKS

I watched Little Man as he scooted into his seat beside two other little boys. He sat for awhile with a stony face looking out the window; then, evidently accepting the fact that the book in front of him was the best that he could expect, he turned and opened it. But as he stared at the book's inside cover, his face clouded, changing from sulky acceptance to puzzlement. His brows furrowed. Then his eyes grew wide, and suddenly he sucked in his breath and sprang from his chair like a wounded animal, flinging the book onto the floor and stomping madly upon it.

Miss Crocker rushed to Little Man and grabbed him up in powerful hands. She shook him vigorously, then set him on the floor again. "Now, just what's gotten into you, Clayton Chester?"

But Little Man said nothing. He just stood staring down at the open book, shivering with indignant anger.

"Pick it up," she ordered.

"No!" defied Little Man.

"No! I'll give you ten seconds to pick up that book, boy, or I'm going to get my switch."

Little Man bit his lower lip, and I knew that he was not going to pick up the book. Rapidly, I turned to the inside cover of my own book and saw immediately what had made Little Man so furious. Stamped on the inside cover was a chart which read:

PROPERTY OF THE BOARD OF EDUCATION
Spokane County, Mississippi
September, 1922

CHRONOLOGICAL ISSUANCE	DATE OF ISSUANCE	CONDITION OF BOOK	RACE OF STUDENT
1	September 1922	New	White
2	September 1923	Excellent	White
3	September 1924	Excellent	White
4	September 1925	Very Good	White
5	September 1926	Good	White
6	September 1927	Good	White
7	September 1928	Average	White
8	September 1929	Average	White
9	September 1930	Average	White
10	September 1931	Poor	White
11	September 1932	Poor	White
12	September 1933	Very Poor	nigra
13			
14			
15			

The blank lines continued down to line 20 and I knew that they had all been reserved for black students. A knot of anger swelled in my throat and held there. But as Miss Crocker directed Little Man to bend over the "whipping" chair, I put aside my anger and jumped up.

"Miz Crocker, don't, please!" I cried. Miss Crocker's dark eyes warned me not to say another word. "I know why he done it!"

"You want part of this switch, Cassie!"

"No'm," I said hastily. "I just wanna tell you how come Little Man done what he done."

"Sit down!" she ordered as I hurried toward her with the open book in my hand.

Holding the book up to her, I said, "See, Miz Crocker, see what it says. They give us these ole books when they didn't want 'em no more."

She regarded me impatiently, but did not look at the book. "Now how could he know what it says? He can't read."

"Yes'm, he can. He been reading since he was four. He can't read all them big words, but he can read them columns. See what's in the last row. Please look, Miz Crocker."

This time Miss Crocker did look, but her face did not change. Then, holding up her head, she gazed unblinkingly down at me.

"S-see what they called us," I said, afraid she had not seen.

"That's what you are," she said coldly. "Now go sit down."

I shook my head, realizing now that Miss Crocker did not even know what I was talking about. She had looked at the page and had understood nothing.

"I said sit down, Cassie!"

I started slowly toward my desk, but as the hickory stick sliced the tense air, I turned back around. "Miz Crocker," I said, "I don't want my book neither."

The switch landed hard upon Little Man's upturned bottom. Miss Crocker looked questioningly at me as I reached up to her desk and placed the book upon it. Then she swung the switch five more times and, discovering that Little Man had no intention of crying, ordered him up.

"All right, Cassie," she sighed, turning to me, "come on and get yours."

By the end of the school day I decided that I would tell Mama everything before Miss Crocker had a chance to do so. From nine years of trial and error, I had learned that punishment was always less severe when I poured out the whole truth to Mama on my own before she had heard anything from anyone else. I knew that Miss Crocker had not spoken to Mama during the lunch period, for she had spent the whole hour in the classroom preparing for the afternoon session.

Mama's classroom was in the back. I crept silently along the quiet hall and peeped cautiously into the open doorway. Mama, pushing a strand of her long, crinkly hair back into the chignon at the base of her slender neck, was seated at her desk watching Miss Crocker thrust a book before her. "Just look at that, Mary," Miss Crocker said, thumping the book twice with her forefinger. "A perfectly good book ruined. Look at that broken binding and those foot marks all over it."

Mama did not speak as she studied the book.

"And here's the one Cassie wouldn't take," she said, placing a second book on Mama's desk with an

outraged slam. "At least she didn't have a tantrum and stomp all over hers. I tell you, Mary, I just don't know what got into those children today. I always knew Cassie was rather high-strung, but Little Man! He's always such a perfect little gentleman."

Mama glanced at the book I had rejected and opened the front cover so that the offensive pages of both books faced her. "You say Cassie said it was because of this front page that she and Little Man didn't want the books?" Mama asked quietly.

"Yes, ain't that something!" Miss Crocker said, forgetting her teacher-training-school diction in her indignation. "The very idea! That's on all the books, and why they got so upset about it I'll never know."

"You punish them?" asked Mama, glancing up at Miss Crocker.

"Well, I certainly did! Whipped both of them good with my hickory stick. Wouldn't you have?" When Mama did not reply, she added defensively, "I had a perfect right to."

"Of course you did, Daisy," Mama said, turning back to the books again. "They disobeyed you." But her tone was so quiet and noncommittal that I knew Miss Crocker was not satisfied with her reaction.

"Well, I thought you would've wanted to know, Mary, in case you wanted to give them a piece of your mind also."

Mama smiled up at Miss Crocker and said rather absently, "Yes, of course, Daisy. Thank you." Then she opened her desk drawer and pulled out some paper, a pair of scissors, and a small brown bottle.

Miss Crocker, dismayed by Mama's seeming unconcern for the seriousness of the matter, thrust her shoulders back and began moving away from the desk. "You understand that if they don't have those books to study from, I'll have to fail them in both reading and composition, since I plan to base all my lessons around — " She stopped abruptly and stared in amazement at Mama. "Mary, what in the world are you doing?"

Mama did not answer. She had trimmed the paper to the size of the books and was now dipping a grey-looking glue from the brown bottle onto the inside cover of one of the books. Then she took the paper and placed it over the glue.

"Mary Logan, do you know what you're doing? That book belongs to the county. If somebody from the superintendent's office ever comes down here and sees that book, you'll be in real trouble."

Mama laughed and picked up the other book. "In the first place no one cares enough to come down here, and in the second place if anyone should come, maybe he could see all the things we need — current books for all of our subjects, not just somebody's old throwaways, desks, papers, blackboards, erasers, maps, chalk. . ." Her voice trailed off as she glued the second book.

"Biting the hand that feeds you. That's what you're doing, Mary Logan, biting the hand that feeds you."

Again Mama laughed. "If that's the case, Daisy, I don't think I need that little bit of food." With the second book finished, she stared at a small pile of seventh-grade books on her desk.

"Well, I just think you're spoiling those children, Mary. They've got to learn how things are sometime."

"Maybe so," said Mama, "but that doesn't mean they have to accept them . . . and maybe we don't either."

Later that week, Cassie's mother is visited in her classroom by three members of the school board. Cassie watches them through a window. Her brother Stacey is a student in their mother's class.

AN UNWELCOME VISIT

Mama seemed startled to see the men, but when Mr. Granger said, "Been hearing 'bout your teaching, Mary, so as members of the school board we thought we'd come by and learn something," she merely nodded and went on with her lesson. Mr. Wellever, the principal, left the room, returning shortly with three folding chairs for the visitors; he himself remained standing.

Mama was in the middle of history and I knew that was bad. I could tell my brother Stacey knew it too; he sat tense near the back of the room, his lips very tight, his eyes on the men. But Mama did not flinch; she always started her history class the first thing in the morning when the students were most alert, and I knew that the hour was not yet up. To make matters worse, her lesson for the day was slavery. She spoke on the cruelty of it; of the rich economic cycle it generated as slaves produced the raw products for the factories of the North and Europe; how the country profited and grew from the free labor of a people still not free.

Before she had finished, Mr. Granger picked up a student's book, flipped it open to the pasted-over front cover, and pursed his lips. "Thought these books belonged to the county," he said, interrupting her. Mama glanced over at him, but did not reply. Mr. Granger turned the pages, stopped, and read something. "I don't see all them things you're teaching in here."

"That's because they're not in there," Mama said.

"Well, if it ain't in here, then you got no right teaching it. This book's approved by the Board of Education and you're expected to teach what's in it."

"I can't do that."

"And why not!"

Mama, her back straight and her eyes fixed on the men, answered, "Because all that's in that book isn't true."

Mr. Granger stood. He laid the book back on the student's desk and headed for the door. The other board member and Kaleb Wallace followed. At the door Mr. Granger stopped and pointed at Mama. "You must be some kind of smart, Mary, to know more than the fellow who wrote that book. Smarter than the school board, too, I reckon."

Mama remained silent, and Mr. Wellever gave her no support.

"In fact," Mr. Granger continued, putting on his hat, "you so smart I expect you'd best just forget about teaching altogether . . . then thataway you'll have plenty of time to write your own book." With that he turned his back on her, glanced at Mr. Wellever to make sure his meaning was clear, and left with the others behind him.

UNIT 7

WORKING

Sadie Frowne

by William Loren Katz
and Jacqueline Hunt Katz

My mother and I came to the United States from Poland when I was a little over thirteen years of age. Two years ago I came to this place, Brownsville, in Brooklyn, New York, where I have friends. I work in a factory making underskirts — all sorts of cheap underskirts, like cotton and calico for the summer and woolen for the winter, but never the silk, satin, or velvet underskirts. I started off earning $4.50 a week and lived on $2 a week.

I got a room in the house of some friends who lived near the factory. I paid $1 a week for the room and was allowed to do light housekeeping — that is, cook my meals in it. I got my own breakfast in the morning, just a cup of coffee and a roll, and at noontime I came home to dinner and took a plate of soup and a slice of bread with the lady of the house. My food for a week cost a dollar, and I had the rest of my money to do as I liked. Now I'm earning $5.50 a week, and will probably get another increase soon.

The factory is in the third story of a brick building. It is in a room twenty feet long and fourteen wide. There are fourteen machines in it. I, and the daughter of the people with whom I live, work two of these machines. The other operators are all men, some young and some old.

At first a few of the young men were rude. When they passed me they would touch my hair and talk about my eyes and my red cheeks, and make jokes. I cried, and said that if they did not stop, I would leave the place. The boss said that that should not be, that no one must annoy me. Some of the other men stood up for me, especially Henry, who said two or three times that he wanted to fight. Now the men all treat me very nicely. It was just that some of them did not know better, not being educated.

Henry is tall and dark, and he has a small mustache. His eyes are brown and large. He is pale and much educated, having been to school. He knows a great many things and has some money saved. I think nearly $400. He is not going to be in a sweatshop all the time, but will soon be in the real estate business, because a lawyer that knows him well has promised to open an office and pay him to manage it.

Henry has seen me home every night for a long time. He wants me to marry him, but I am not seventeen yet, and I think that is too young. He is only nineteen, so we can wait.

I have been to the fortune teller's three or four times,

and she always tells me that though I have had such a lot of trouble I am to be very rich and happy. I believe her because she has told so many things that have come true. So I will keep working in the factory for a time. Of course it is hard, but I would have to work hard even if I was married.

At seven o'clock we all sit down to our machines and the boss brings to each one the pile of work that he or she is to finish during the day, what they call in English their "stint." This pile is put down beside the machine and as soon as a skirt is done it is laid on the other side of the machine. Sometimes the work is not all finished by six o'clock and then the one who is behind must work over-time. Sometimes one is finished ahead of time and gets away at four or five o'clock, but generally we are not done till six o'clock.

The machines go like mad all day, because the faster you work the more money you get. Sometimes in my haste I get my finger caught and the needle goes right through it. It goes so quick, though, that it does not hurt much. I bind the finger up with a piece of cotton and go on working. We all have accidents like that. Where the needle goes through the nail, it makes a sore finger, or where it splinters a bone, it does much harm. Sometimes a finger has to come off. Generally, though, one can be cured by a salve.

All the time we are working the boss walks about examining the finished garments and making us do them over again if they are not just right. So we have to be careful as well as swift. But I am getting so good at the work that within a year I will be making $7 a week, and then I can save at least $3.50 a week. I have over $200 saved now.

For the last two winters I have been going to night school at Public School 84 on Glenmore Avenue. I have learned reading, writing, and arithmetic. I can read quite well in English now and I look at the newspapers every day. I read English books, too, sometimes.

I am going back to night school again this winter. Plenty of my friends go there. Some of the women in my class are more than forty years of age. Like me, they did not have a chance to learn anything in the old country. It is good to have an education; it makes you feel higher. Ignorant people are all low. People say now that I am clever and fine in conversation.

We have just finished a strike in our business. It spread all over and the United Brotherhood of Garment Workers was in it. That takes in the cloakmakers, coatmakers, and all the others. We struck for shorter hours, and after being out four weeks, won the fight. Now, we only have to work nine and a half hours a day, and we get the same pay as before. So the Union does good after all, in spite of what some people say against it — that it just takes our money and does nothing. I pay 25 cents a month to the union. I do not mind that because it is for our benefit. The next strike is going to be for a raise of wages, which we all ought to have. There is a little expense for charity, too. If any worker is injured or sick, we all give money to help.

I have many friends and we often have jolly parties. Many of the young men like to talk to me, but I don't go out with any except Henry.

Lately he has been urging me more and more to get married — but I think I'll wait.

Bread and Roses

by James Oppenheim

As we come marching, marching, in the beauty
of the day,
A million darkened kitchens, a thousand mill
lofts gray,
Are touched with all the radiance that a sudden
sun discloses,
For the people hear us singing, "Bread and
roses! Bread and roses!"

As we come marching, marching, we battle too
for men,
For they are women's children and we mother
them again.
Our lives shall not be sweated from birth until
life closes.
Hearts starve as well as bodies:
Give us bread,
but give us roses!

As we come marching, marching, unnumbered
women dead
Go crying through our singing their ancient cry
for bread.
Small art and love and beauty their drudging
spirits knew.
Yes, it is bread we fight for — but we fight for
roses, too!

As we come marching, marching, we bring the
greater days.
The rising of the women means the rising of
the race.
No more the drudge and idler — ten that toil
where one reposes,
But a sharing of life's glories: Bread and roses!
Bread and roses!

The Ladies' Underground 1866-1870

by Dorothy Nafus Morrison

PORTLAND, the largest town on the Willamette, had eight thousand inhabitants who lived in small frame houses along a zigzag scattering of paths. Trees had been cut to make room for the town, jagged stumps stood everywhere, and a dark forest crowded in on three sides. Abigail swept down the board walks under the broad rooflike awnings, past the stores, saloons, and Chinese laundries, to the office of Jacob Mayer, wholesaler. Heart beating fast, she asked for a stock of goods on credit for her new millinery and notions store.

"Won't some of your friends go security for you?" he asked, not unkindly.

"My husband went broke going security, and I vowed long ago that I would never copy his mistake," she replied with spirit.

"How much of a stock do you want?"

Abigail hesitated. She might as well ask for a lot. "About . . . about a hundred dollars will do for a beginning," she hazarded, her voice trembling.

Mr. Mayer chuckled. "Nonsense! You could carry home a hundred dollars' worth of millinery in a silk apron. Let me select you a stock of goods."

Humming, he bustled around his warehouse and laid out silk and feathers and artificial flowers until the bill totaled one thousand two hundred dollars.

Abigail looked longingly at it. "I'm afraid to risk it," she said, although she was tempted, for it would really

Abigail holding Clyde in 1867.

make a fine shop. She offered him her thirty dollars in part payment.

Mr Mayer refused. "Never mind. You'll need that money. Take this stock home and do the best you can with it. Then come back and get some more."

In three weeks she was back — with money to pay off her debt. This time she took three thousand dollars' worth of stock, again on credit, and again she soon paid it off. The Duniway store was under way.

Before long Abigail began to burn at tales her customers told.

One mother had been deserted by a husband who sold the household goods and left town. Now she had a chance to buy some furniture and rent a house cheaply.

"If I could borrow the money in a lump sum, I could repay it in installments," she said between sobs. "Then I could keep my children together, with the aid of a few boarders."

Later that day, when a friend dropped in, Abigail told him the story. "I'll loan her the money," he said heartily. "She can give me a mortgage on the furniture."

As soon as she could leave the store, Abigail went to the meager home with the good news. All went well until the husband returned and would not let her pay the mortgage. He had the law on his side. The good friend was out his money. The woman sued for divorce. The home was broken up, children scattered.

"It was wrong — wrong," thought Abigail. "A woman's business should be her own. With laws as they were, a woman was at the mercy of her husband, and little more than a slave."

Another day, Abigail was working on a twenty-dollar bonnet for a wealthy client. She looked out the shop window and saw a well-to-do farmer riding by on one horse, and proudly leading a fine racing animal which he had just bought. He couldn't sit more erect, Abigail thought, if he'd swallowed a yardstick.

Sometime later his wife came in, followed by two little girls and carrying a baby in her arms.

"I've come to see it I could get a job of plain sewing," the mother said timidly. "I am obliged to earn some money."

"I'm sorry," Abigail replied, and explained that when she had extra work, she gave it to those in need.

Weeping, the woman said, "I promised these girls that if they would work hard and make lots of butter, I'd buy them waterproof suits to wear to Sunday school." Tears streamed down her face. "But he used the butter money to help pay for his new race horse."

"I'll sell you the goods and charge the bill to your husband," Abigail offered.

"John won't allow me to go in debt," replied the woman. Although Abigail offered to cut and fit the suits without charge, the woman refused, drew the blankets around the baby, and left.

Abigail sizzled. Women worked, just as men did. They ought to have some say in how the money was spent, some money of their own.

A year later, when the woman died, the minister preached a funeral sermon consoling the bereaved husband. Abigail thought long and deeply about the butter money, the "defrauded children," the dead wife, and the thoroughbred race horse.

Still again, a man came in with his wife and four little girls, and the mother selected four fashionable hats for them.

"What's the damage?" the man asked with gruff humor.

WOMEN PAY TAXES!!

WOMEN OBEY THE LAWS!

Women and Children suffer from dirty streets, impure milk, adulterated food, bad sanitary conditions, smoke laden air, underpaid labor.

WOMEN CLEAN THE HOMES:
LET THEM HELP CLEAN THE CITY

VOTE	300 X 'YES'	AMENDMENT NO. 1, NOV. 5, 1912

It will give the women A SQUARE DEAL.
It will give your girl the same chance
as your boy.

VOTES FOR WOMEN

COLLEGE EQUAL SUFFRAGE LEAGUE. 406 SELLING BLDG

"Four hats at three dollars each, will be twelve dollars," Abigail replied.

The man's smile turned to a frown. He demanded something cheaper, and finally chose some bark hats which Abigail kept for berry pickers. The children were disappointed, and one said, "He thinks silver-mounted harness isn't a bit too good for his horses, though."

The mother silenced the child, smiled sweetly at her husband, and after sending him on an errand, had Abigail package the fashionable hats.

"When he comes back, he'll pay you the price of the bark hats," she said, pulling some coins from her pocket. "Here's four dollars and a half. When I come to town again, I'll bring you the rest."

Abigail was puzzled. "Won't your husband notice the difference when he sees the hats?"

"No!" the woman replied sharply. "He doesn't know any more about a hat than I do about a horse collar!"

A few days later Abigail told another storekeeper about the hats. "Do you think I'll ever see the rest of the money?" she asked.

"Of course!" he replied with a chuckle. "We couldn't make any profit on fancy goods if it wasn't for what the women steal from their husbands."

Steal! From their husbands! Women were reduced to that; Abigail was aghast.

Her shop became a center where women came not only to buy, but to talk with the sympathetic Mrs. Duniway. She heard dozens of stories about injustice under the law, which she helped if she could. She lent goods to set up small shops, and at least once she lost her investment because the wife's business was taken to pay an old debt of the long-absent husband, a debt incurred before marriage. She didn't dislike men. Quite the contrary, she had many men friends, and often persuaded them to help, too.

One day an acquaintance burst into her shop. "Mrs. Duniway!" she exclaimed. "I want you to go with me to the courthouse!"

"The courthouse is a place for men," Abigail replied. "Can't you get some man to go with you?"

"They all say they are too busy." The woman explained that her husband had died without a will, leaving it almost impossible for her to get enough of his estate to live on.

At first Abigail refused to go, but at last, half ashamed, she put on her hat.

"Only think!" said the woman as they hurried along the street. "My husband — if he had lived and I had died — could have spent every dollar we had earned in twenty years of married life, and nobody would have cared. My girls and I have sold butter, eggs, poultry, cord wood, vegetables, grain and hay — almost enough to pay the taxes and meet all of our bills, but I can't even buy a pair of shoe strings without being lectured by the court."

Abigail told the woman's story to the judge, who granted the immediate request, though he couldn't change the law. But back at the shop, while she worked on expensive bonnets for her well-to-do customers, she brooded. Unfairness again. Things ought to be changed.

That night at dinner she told her husband the story. "Ben, Ben," she said. "One half of the women are dolls, the rest of them are drudges, and we're all fools!"

Ben placed his hand on her head. "Don't you know it will never be any better for women until they have the right to vote?" he gently asked.

"What good would that do?"

"Can't you see? Women do half the work. They ought to control half the pay," Ben replied. "If they voted, they would soon be lawmakers."

Abigail stared, feeling as if a light had been turned on. Lawmakers! If women could make the laws! Things could be changed! Maybe it was up to her to start something.

ALICIA ALONSO

Adapted by Jamila Gastón Colón

Alicia Alonso is my name. I love to dance. I am a ballerina who lives in Cuba. I was born in 1921, many years before your parents were born.

When I was a little girl there was no ballet in Cuba. My work has helped to make ballet popular. Today thousands of Cuban children study ballet.

The parents of some of my friends in Havana hired a Russian ballet master, Nikolai Yavorsky, to teach us to dance. He taught us on a large, open stage in a building called Pro Arte Musical. Everything was new, the building, the teacher and the idea of ballet for Cuban children.

I loved ballet from the beginning. I loved to practice the steps and movements for hours. My mother and father were very surprised.

I come from a long line of Spanish-Cuban families. The family goes back to Spain's colony at St. Augustine, Florida, which was the first European settlement in the New World. My father was very proud of his ancestry. He taught his children the traditions of Spain. He was very strict and set many rules. He believed that men belonged in the outside world, that they should go to college and have careers. He believed that women were weak and must remain at home to be protected. My father thought my sister and I should finish secondary school and then think about marriage and a family.

My mother was a cheerful woman who loved music and had developed her talent for embroidery. She made my first ballet costumes. She trained other women in Cuba to make tutus (ballet skirts) for our performances. It was my mother who entered my sister and me in ballet and drama classes at Pro Arte.

I was the youngest of four children. I had a sister and two brothers. They taught me the popular Cuban dance, the *son* and the *danzonete*. I also liked the African beat of the *rumba* and the *conga*. Afro-Cuban rhythms reached the city from the interior of the island. The people played conga drums and bongos.

My teacher, Nikolai Yavorsky, was very strict and tough. Once during a dance we were rehearsing, another

girl had to throw a balloon to me. I missed it, and Mister
Yavorsky became very angry. He slammed the balloon
on my head. I was not hurt, but I was very upset. My
sister, Cuca, who was in the class told him that we were
going home. Later Mr. Yavorsky apologized to us but
Cuca insisted that he must say he was sorry in front of
the whole class. He did. I was glad because now I could
continue my ballet classes. "Backs flat, straight, shoulders down. No, not back, down, necks up. Relax."

In lesson after lesson I listened carefully, learning
this new language of dance. My legs were strong, and I
was graceful. Ballet felt wonderful.

There were no books to read about ballet dancers, so
Mr. Yavorsky often told us stories of dancers like Pav-
lova, Nijinsky and many others.

By the time I was thirteen there were boys in my
ballet class. Many years later I married Fernando, one of
the young men who had studied ballet. When I was fifteen
years old, I left Cuba and went to the United States. Fernando and I were married there and I had a baby,
Laurita.

I was very shy. It was hard to understand English.
We lived in New York City where people from many
countries make their home. My first dance teacher in
New York was Enrico. When I did not understand the
spoken word I learned by watching. Fernando spoke English and he helped me.

Fernando got a job dancing at Jones Beach. I liked to

practice with him while Laurita, our baby, watched. One day the director saw me dance and offered me a job. I began teaching children at Jones Beach. I also made my debut on the American stage at Jones Beach, where I appeared with two men as partners.

Soon afterwards I danced in a Broadway play and continued to study ballet. Fernando also worked. We both danced. Soon we joined a small company.

When I was nineteen, I discovered I had a peculiar tendency to bump into things. Fernando used to tease me about it. It even happened during a performance. One time I became very sick and dizzy, and I saw spots in front of my eyes. My friends helped me off the stage. The doctor said I had to have surgery on my right eye. It turned out I needed two eye operations. After the operations, Fernando, Laurita and I went home to Cuba for a rest.

My family in Cuba took me to see an eye doctor called an ophthalmologist. He told me I needed surgery again — on both eyes! And my tonsils had to be removed! After the operations I had to stay in bed for months and not move a muscle. During the first few months, weights were placed around my head at night to make sure I did not move it during sleep. My doctors concluded that I could never dance again. I was nineteen years old, which is still very young. This news made me very, very unhappy.

In the weeks and months of lying still in bed, I danced in my imagination. I rehearsed daily in my head and with my fingertips. I worked particularly hard on one ballet,

GISELLE. I realized then that dancing was my life, I could not stop. Everyday I listened to music, and my fingers leaped and bent to the movements of the ballet. The bed sheet was my stage and Fernando corrected the errors. My fingers became very quick and nimble.

When the bandages were removed, I had lost a great deal of my eyesight. In my right eye, images looked as if I were seeing them through a scratched window pane. In my left eye, I lost my vision on one side. This was the worst thing that could have happened to me. A dancer must be able to see in order to learn. I also had to conquer my fear. I could not see into space the way I used to.

When I started to get around, I could only move very slowly. I was stiff after not dancing for a year. I found a rehearsal room in a Havana studio where I had studied as a little girl, and I began to work. Little by little I regained my strength. I learned to walk again. My first jumps were small but they caused great pain in my legs.

I worked hard to see into space with my changed vision. Only by working each day slowly, going over exercises time after time, could I learn to dance and move gracefully again. Little by little, I learned to pirouette and make soaring leaps. My patience and determination would do justice to Beethoven, my favorite composer. He wrote some of his greatest music after becoming totally deaf.

Gradually I expanded my activities. I joined a group of writers, composers, dancers and other creative artists who met together to talk and to pool abilities. They encouraged me to create dances, that is, to choreograph. My first ballet as a choreographer was LA CONDESITA. Soon I was teaching a dance class. These activities brought me closer to dancing for a performance.

After a while I returned to New York. Once more there were classes and rehearsals. I continued to work very hard. Soon many newspapers and magazines published my picture and said many kind things about my work. They called my dancing "brilliant." When there was no work in New York I returned to Havana, Cuba. I invited American dancers to come, too.

In Havana, I formed a company called Ballet Alicia Alonso. Sixteen members were Cuban and the rest were from the United States. We rehearsed the ballets GISELLE, PETROUCHKA and COPELIA. We learned new ballets. There was little money but we felt great enthusiasm for our work. Soon I arranged for us to tour South America. There was so little money that many times my mother made and repaired our costumes. Once she made a costume for me from curtains in our hotel room. All Fernando and I wanted to do was to keep dancing. I kept learning new ways to dance. I was invited to many countries to perform, including the Soviet Union.

In 1959 there was a revolution in Cuba. After this change in the government, I traveled back and forth freely between the United States and Cuba. I performed as a guest artist with Ballet Russe de Monte Carlo and the American Ballet Theater.

The new Cuban government gave my Cuban ballet company money to support our work. Cubans had been extremely poor with little opportunity for education. I wanted to bring this culture to my people.

I helped bring ballet to workers in small towns and to children in schools. My daughter, Laura Alonso, helped me to develop ways to work with people in hospitals. Other dancers helped too.

We joined in the life of the people of my country by joining work brigades to help harvest vegetables, and we also helped patrol the streets.

Many years after surgery on my eyes, I became increasingly blind. I lost almost all sense of space and I had to depend on the images in my mind. It was very hard for me. In order for me to leap through the air, the other dancers on the stage made a tapping sound so I would know where to move. My friends in the United States did not know about my blindness or my work with the Cuban people for many years.

When I could barely see a pinpoint of light, I had to have another eye operation. After it I could not dance for two years. They were the saddest years of my life. In November, 1974, I was given the Ana Betancourt award, named after Cuba's first woman fighter for women's rights. At the ceremony, I surprised everyone by dancing.

I have been given a great deal of recognition and many awards for my dancing.

In 1975, I was invited to dance again in the United States. I had not been there in fifteen years. The audience in New York made me feel very welcome. They shouted "bienvenida" which means "welcome."

The Ballet Nacional de Cuba made its first appearance in New York at the Metropolitan Opera House. In the company of eighty-five people were my grandson Ivan, a corps member, and my daughter, Laura, a ballet mistress.

I continue to dance. My body demands it, and so does my mind. Someone asked me why I stay in Cuba when people all over the world love my dancing. I answered, "By staying in Cuba I gained the love of my people. And who has that is very rich."

UNIT 8

BREAKING BARRIERS

When Valerie Grows Up

BY NORMA KLEIN

When Valerie grows up, she is going to be an astronaut. Or she might be an artist like her mother. Maybe she'll be a mother, too, but only if she can have a girl.

"What did you want to be when you were little?" she asks Mrs. Weiss, the baby sitter.

"I always wanted to be a concert pianist," Mrs. Weiss says, "and that is what I became."

"You mean you did it? How come you don't do it now?"

"Because I got married and had children."

"So?"

"So, you cannot do both. The piano takes too much from you."

"Oh," Valerie says.

"In my day it was different," Mrs. Weiss says. "You did not do both."

A lot of things were different in Mrs. Weiss's day, evidently. Valerie looks at Mrs. Weiss and tries to imagine her playing the piano on a stage like that man they saw on TV. "Did you play on a stage?" she asks.

"Many times," Mrs. Weiss says.

"Were you nervous?"

"Always."

It's so hard to imagine. Valerie is lying on her back with her legs in the air. "Don't you miss it?" she asks suddenly.

"Of course I do," says Mrs. Weiss.

That makes Valerie feel bad. If playing the piano was what Mrs. Weiss liked to do, that is what she should have done. It isn't fair. "I'm going to be an astronaut," Valerie says. "I want to go to the moon."

"Not me," says Mrs. Weiss. "I wouldn't go up in a rocket if you paid me."

"You wouldn't?" That seems funny to Valerie. She would go up in a rocket in a minute, but she would never have the courage to play the piano in front of a whole lot of people she didn't know. People seem to be completely different about what makes them scared.

In the park one day, one of Mrs. Weiss's friends, another lady, says to Marco, "What do you want to be when you grow up?"

"A dancer," says Marco.

The lady laughs. "You can't be! You're a boy."

"There are too men dancers," says Valerie. "Our mother took us to see *The Nutcracker Suite* and they had men."

"Oh well," the lady says.

"I want to jump way up high," Marco says.

"I bet you'll be a doctor and take care of sick people and make them better," the lady says.

"I want to be a dancer," Marco says. He jumps to show her.

"He can if he wants," Valerie says.

"They always change their minds," the lady says to Mrs. Weiss. "He's too little to know what he's talking about."

Valerie feels mad at that lady. She's not so smart herself. She didn't even know there were men dancers. She probably never even went to the ballet. Grownups think they know so much, but they don't. If Marco is a dancer, Valerie will go and see him. She will get free tickets and sit in the first row. If he jumps very very high, she will yell, "Bravo!" That's what you have to yell if you like it.

Space Sisters

by Lauri Welles

They whizzed past the rings of Saturn (which were so beautiful!) and zoomed right out of the solar system. Then the starship went into a space warp and came out among many faraway stars. They saw, up close, the Big and Little Dippers, white giant stars and stars called red dwarfs. They saw a nova, which is the birth of a star. The pilot even tried to show them a black hole in space, but it was much too dangerous. They went halfway across the universe and back, stopping at one of Earth's space stations on their return. Finally, just when they were beginning to get tired and hungry, the captain told them to fasten their seatbelts. Touchdown was to be in four minutes.

"What an incredible trip!" Stephanie thought. Even though the class was now back at school, she was so excited, she couldn't keep her mind on anything else. "I just love the Planetarium!" she said to her friend Hilary, who was standing on line with her in the cafeteria. "I'm so excited, I don't even think I can eat," she continued. "Don't you think that was absolutely the best class trip ever?"

Hilary shrugged. "I guess," she said, looking at the menu written on the blackboard. "I'm starving. I'll eat your lunch if you don't want it."

"You're always starving." Stephanie wrinkled her nose impatiently. "All you ever think about is food."

"Well, I'm too skinny." Hilary was very matter-of-fact.

"You're really a bottomless pit. Still, I have to get a sandwich for Becky — she's saving our table. And I suppose I'll get something, too. Oh," Stephanie took some food, then stopped and sighed, "I hope we go back to

the Planetarium soon. I swear, someday, I'll go to outer space. I think I've decided, I'm going to be an astronaut."

A loud voice behind Stephanie suddenly exclaimed, "Hey, did you hear that? Attention, everybody!" Ricky, a boy in their fifth grade class, had been standing nearby and listening in. He announced, "Stephanie Brown is going to be the first American woman astronaut!"

Stephanie cringed, then straightened her shoulders. "There already are American women astronauts," she said. "And anyway, maybe I will be one."

"Oh, excuse me, Commander — I mean, Miss Astronaut," said Ricky, saluting.

Stephanie gritted her teeth. She hated boys like Ricky. She picked up the lunch tray, lifted her chin proudly and marched away, joining Becky and Hilary at their table.

"Ricky's such a creep," Stephanie said, sitting. "I told him I want to be an astronaut," she started. But before she could explain what had happened, something flew at her from behind. It was a paper missile, labelled "U.S. Starship Stupid Stephanie," and it was from Ricky.

Becky picked it up and unfolded it. "There's typing inside. I think it's some kind of announcement. But it's hard to read, because there are a lot of long words."

Stephanie said, "Let me try. Umm . . . National contest, students eighteen years and under. Projects related to study of space. Examples . . ." She stopped. "Oh, it is really hard."

"Maybe I can help," suggested Hilary.

Together, the three girls figured out the Planetarium was holding a space-science contest. "Hey, look at this," Stephanie read. "First prize: $3,000 and a trip to Cape Canaveral, all expenses paid!"

Becky sat up straight. "Three thousand dollars!"

"And a trip!" Hilary stopped eating. "Wow."

Stephanie was already making plans. "I'd give the money to poor people. But Cape Canaveral — maybe I could get on the astronauts list!"

"What astronauts list?" asked Hilary.

"The list of future astronauts. They must have one," Stephanie replied. "I wonder what sort of project I could do."

"Maybe you could build a model," suggested Becky.

"Yes!" Stephanie became excited, "like of a space station, and tell what it would be like to live there. Do you think building a model is hard?"

"You could ask Maria," Hilary suggested, standing. "Maria's always building things. She could probably give you lots of advice. I'm going to get dessert."

"I'll go with you." Becky cleared off the empty plates. "If you'd like, Steph, I'll try to find Maria."

"That would be great!" Stephanie said. "Thanks." She stared at the announcement and daydreamed while her friends were gone. Imagine growing up on a space station; for vacations, taking trips to Mars . . .

When Hilary and Becky returned, they had Maria and a girl Stephanie didn't know with them.

Maria said, "Stephanie, that's really a hot idea! I'd love to help." She introduced the new girl. "This is Susel. She's in the other fifth grade. She has a sister in college who's a space whiz."

"Not especially space, just a major in science," Susel corrected Maria. "Hello, Stephanie. I'm sure my sister would love to help, too. Why don't you and Maria come over Saturday morning?"

"Terrific!" agreed Stephanie.

Maria frowned. "I'd really like to, but I can't Saturday. A cousin of mine just moved in with us for the rest of the year, and Saturday, I'm supposed to try to help her make friends."

"How old is she?" Becky asked.

"About our age," Maria replied. "She'll go to school here, probably starting next week."

"Maybe we could be her friends, then." Becky smiled. Stephanie nodded.

"That's right," agreed Susel. "Bring her along with you. And Becky, you and Hilary come, too."

Hilary poked Stephanie. "That way we can all help old 'Step-on-me'; she probably needs it." Stephanie made a face. "Well, you know you're not practical," said Hilary.

"And you're *too* practical," retorted Stephanie, poking Hilary back. "The Practical Pit."

"I'll see you Saturday then?" asked Susel. "Maria knows where I live."

When Hilary, Becky and Stephanie arrived at Susel's on Saturday, Maria and her cousin, Isabella, were already there.

"Isabella's a little shy," Maria announced. Isabella blushed.

Susel laughed. "What an introduction!"

Becky agreed. "You're being embarrassing."

"Am I?" asked Maria. Her cousin blushed more at that and nodded. But Maria went on. "It's the truth, though. You can see she's not at all like me — I'm strong stuff!"

Stephanie studied the two of them. They weren't alike. She looked at the others. In fact, no one in the group was. She grinned, thinking, "This is fun; we're a great group—assorted nuts!"

Susel stood up. "There's milk and cookies. Stephanie, I'm sorry. My sister can't be here. But she liked your idea. She left some suggestions — a list of the things you might do. See."

Stephanie read the list with growing horror. There seemed to be a million things on it! "This is terrible!" She exclaimed. "I can't do all this."

"You don't have to do them all. Only the important ones, on the bottom." Susel pointed to the sheet. "And my sister said for the science parts, she'd give you books and other advice."

"But even still! Just look at this! I'd have to write about how they grow their food. I'd have to write about what kind of work they do — probably about government and laws; about what living in space does to people's bodies — "

Maria interrupted. "The deadline's more than two months away."

Stephanie put down the paper. "It's still impossible. It's just too much."

"My father grows vegetables. I could probably find out about the food." Hilary took a handful of cookies.

"That's right, you could," Becky giggled. "He says he has to grow food the way you eat, because otherwise he couldn't afford to pay for it all."

Susel turned to Stephanie. "Hey, besides the science parts, I might be able to help with the laws! My mother is studying to be a lawyer."

Becky said excitedly, "My mother's a paramedic. I

could do the medical parts. We could all work on it together. I'm sure there's something Isabella could do!"

Isabella looked up. Her eyes were shining and there was a big smile on her face for the first time. "I like science. I could help do those parts with Susel's sister. I also love to draw and paint," she added very softly. "Maybe I could draw pictures, sort of illustrations of it all."

"That's right. And I'd be building the model," added Maria. "What do you think, Steph?" asked Becky. "Don't you think it's a fantastic idea?!"

"And we'd all share the $3,000!" chimed in Hilary.

"But there isn't anything left I could do! The rest of you would be doing everything!" exclaimed Stephanie.

Susel had a suggestion. "Maybe you could put it all together, sort of organize things."

"That doesn't seem like much. I wouldn't be doing anything new, on my own."

"But you organized us. You brought us together," said Susel.

"Yes," agreed Becky. "It was your idea in the first place."

Stephanie was still upset, but then she remembered something her mother said. "Hey, I think I know what I can write about!" she said slowly, the thought forming in her head. "It's really important not only what people do, but how they do it, if they get along together, in society. Besides just organizing things, I could write about how people in space might get along, what problems they'd have, maybe even if they'd have fun and things." Now she was excited again. "Wow, this is going to be incredible!" She jumped out of her seat and looked around. The others were giggling. Stephanie realized why. She grinned broadly. "What a fantastic idea I had!"

"When do we start?" asked Isabella.

"Right away."

"We should arrange to meet every week," said Susel. "That way we can report to each other what we learned."

"And Stephanie can organize things," added Maria.

Which is what happened, though it turned out to be not only fantastic but very hard. There were many problems. Maria was supposed to work in her parents' store on weekends. (All the girls decided to help, so it was okay.) The group had to meet in different places all the time. (This was fun actually.) And sometimes they had to take care of Hilary's younger sister (this was the hardest of all, but they found there were ways even she could help).

There were times, too, that the group didn't get along well. It was Hilary, especially, who made problems. She was very bossy and the girls were becoming irritated. They decided Stephanie had to figure out what to do. "Why me?" Stephanie asked. "I know, I know; I'm writing about solving problems. I'm supposed to be the organizer."

So one day, after a meeting, she took Hilary aside. "Listen, Hilary, you've got to stop telling people what to do. You act like you're the boss or something."

Hilary stuck out her chin, "Do you think you are?!"

"No, I don't," said Stephanie. "My mother called this a cooperative group. A co-op, like where your father grows the food, or Susel's apartment house. Anyway, that means working together, without one person telling the others what they should do."

"Right now," Hilary replied, "that's what you're telling me."

"I'm not really telling you." Stephanie thought a moment. "I'm making a suggestion. I'm suggesting that maybe the others will stop liking you if you don't change the way you've been acting."

Hilary looked unhappy at that. "But it's not just me. Everybody, sometimes, has been having at least little fights."

Stephanie nodded. "We're a kind of family, and that happens when families get together. We're sort of like sisters. But, meanwhile, we also have an agreement — that we'll try to cooperate and not act too bossy or anything."

Hilary lowered her head. "I don't mean to be bossy. It's just that sometimes I get excited and I want things to be right — " She bit her lip.

Stephanie touched her arm. "I know. I didn't say I was going to stop liking you."

Hilary looked funny and then, suddenly, laughed. "You know what I just thought of? You know what you said, that we're kind of like sisters? Well, what we are is space-sisters!" She laughed again. "Yeah, space-sisters, that's what we are."

From that point on, Hilary tried to be the most cooperative of all. And although she didn't always succeed, when the others noticed the change, they tried harder themselves. They finished the project just in time, handing it in the day of the deadline.

Now all they could do was wait. "They're going to announce the winners in the newspapers next Saturday," said Stephanie.

"Wow!" exclaimed Becky. "Our names in the newspaper!"

"My parents said to ask everyone to come to our house for a victory party," offered Hilary.

Isabella nudged Maria and whispered something to her. "My parents are expecting you in the store that morning." Maria reminded the group.

Isabella giggled. "That's right," she said. "You promised that you would still be helping out."

Maria continued. "We get the newspapers there first thing in the morning, anyway. There'll be lots of copies. Is 10 a.m. okay?"

The girls looked disappointed, but they sighed and nodded. That was part of their agreement. They had to say yes.

Saturday morning, Hilary and Stephanie arrived at the store together. There was a sign outside: "Closed 10-11 a.m. Private party!"

"Oh, boy!" Hilary knocked excitedly. "Our victory party!"

Maria's mother opened the door. What a surprise!

The whole store was decorated with streamers and balloons, and there was a cake and sodas sitting on the table.

Maria's father stepped forward. "We wanted to thank you girls for helping us out. So we made a little celebration."

Becky and Susel were already there, as were both their parents, Stephanie's mother and Hilary's father! Stephanie was so surprised she couldn't say anything. And, with the exception of Hilary, the others were being very quiet, too.

"We're not the winners," said Maria.

Susel held up a clipping. "We didn't win the prize."

Stephanie stopped dead in her tracks. "You mean we didn't win *first* prize?" she asked.

"We didn't win any prize," Becky said glumly.

"What a gyp. What a victory. What a bunch of winners we are!" Hilary stomped over to a chair and plunked herself down.

"I think you are winners," said her father. "I think you're a bunch of very special people."

"Oh, Daddy you're just saying that." Hilary looked at him and frowned.

"I don't think he is." That was Stephanie's mother. "I've seen my daughter have a victory over her temper. She's also more tolerant of others."

Stephanie was very embarrassed, but she said, "I guess that's true. Except it's not that I'm more tolerant. I just like people better."

"You do," said Hilary. "You are! And maybe now, I'm not so bossy. Also, I have a lot more fun!"

"And Isabella isn't so shy anymore!" Susel exclaimed.

Stephanie's mother smiled. "I think you all feel this

way because you've learned the value of working together. You have a better understanding of one
another's problems — "

"There goes your mother," Hilary interrupted, "lec-
turing again."

Becky quickly piped up. "It's true, though. It's like
now I have a whole group of new friends!"

Maria jumped up. "So do I!"

"So do I!"

"So do I!"

"So do I!" That was all of them!

"Now we really should celebrate!" exclaimed
Maria.

"We're Space Sisters! Party! Party!" Hilary ran over
to the table. "I'm practically starving to death! When do
we eat?!"

WRITE A PETITION

by Siv Widerberg

You may not believe it
but we've got a soccer field now
behind Andy and Hugo's house,
beside the grocery store
in our town outside Stockholm, Sweden
A really neat soccer field
with goalposts and everything
"Write a petition
and tape it up on the door
of every building!" said a big guy I know
So that's what we did
We want a soccer field!
we wrote
And then: Anders Andersson,
Leif Lundin, Hugo Blomkvist,
Gertrud Nilsson (who's me)
and all the others
Last Tuesday we got it,
behind Andy and Hugo's house,
beside the grocery store
and with white goalposts

Try it yourself
and you'll see:
Write down what you want on top,
and then a whole bunch of names underneath it

Anyhow we got
our soccer field
that way
even if you don't believe it!

ILLUSTRATIONS

ILLUSTRATIONS

About the Editors

Ruth S. Meyers, Ph.D., is a reading specialist teacher trainer and feminist political activist. She is an adjunct assistant professor at New York University, Department of Educational Psychology.

Beryle Banfield, Ed.D., is a consultant on curriculum development and a specialist in urban education, African and African American literature. She is president of the Council on Interracial Books for Children.

Jamila Gastón Colón is a teacher specializing in early childhood education. She is a doctoral candidate in multicultural education at the University of Massachusetts at Amherst.

About the Publishers

Founded in 1966, the Council on Interracial Books for Children today raises public awareness to racism, sexism, handicapism and other anti-human values in children's books and learning materials. The Council publishes a regular periodical, the BULLETIN, which is sent to subscribers eight times a year. The Council also operates the Racism and Sexism Resource Center which develops and disseminates print and audiovisual anti-racist and anti-sexist training materials to sensitize students and teachers to bias in school and society (a catalog listing these materials is available free from the Council at 1841 Broadway, New York, N.Y. 10023).

The Council believes that education in a democratic society must encourage young people to recognize social injustice and inspire them with the knowledge that people can work together to achieve social change.

THE FEMINIST PRESS offers alternatives in education and in literature. Founded in 1970, this nonprofit, tax-exempt educational and publishing organization works to eliminate sexual stereotypes in books and schools and to provide literature with a broad vision of human potential. The publishing program includes reprints of important works by women, feminist biographies of women, and nonsexist children's books. Curricular materials, bibliographies, directories, and a quarterly journal provide information and support for students and teachers of women's studies. Inservice projects help to transform teaching methods and curricula. Through publications and projects, The Feminist Press contributes to the rediscovery of the history of women and the emergence of a more humane society. A catalog listing other children's books and bibliographies is available from The Feminist Press, Box 334, Old Westbury, New York 11568.